MW01109341
SINGULARITY
RISE OF THE POSTHUMANS

DAVID MICHELINIE
JENNIE WOOD
NANCY HANSEN
BRANT FOWLER
LEE HOUSTON JR
CHRIS MAGEE
JAIME RAMOS

PRO SE PRESS™

PRO SE PRESS

SINGULARITY: RISE OF THE POSTHUMANS
A Pro Se Publications

Concept by Jaime Ramos
Lord Pemberton's Adjustment Service by David Michelinie
Charada by Jennie Wood
Simon Simple by Nancy Hansen
The Rebel by Lee Houston Jr.
The Eye of the Mind by Brant Fowler
Pistoleer by Chris Magee
The Bride of Dr. Bravo by Jaime Ramos
Editing by Jaime Ramos and Wayne Carey

Cover Art by Rick Johnson
Book Design by Antonino Lo Iacono
New Pulp Logo Design by Sean E. Ali
New Pulp Seal Design by Cari Reese

Pro Se Productions, LLC
133 1/2 Broad Street
Batesville, AR, 72501
870-834-4022

editorinchief@prose-press.com
www.prose-press.com

SINGULARITY: RISE OF THE POSTHUMANS

LORD PEMBERTON'S ADJUSTMENT SERVICE

by
David Michelinie

The Mourning Lads were out and about again, and blood was sure to follow.

William Forrester, Lord Pemberton, pressed his back against the rough brick wall of the alley and watched through oval openings in the red leather that hid his face. There were five—no, six—of the ragtag toughs passing by with crudely tattooed tears dripping from their eyes, marking them for the cutthroat human plague that stalked the less-genteel byways of New Southampton. He knew their tattered shirts and vests would conceal rail spikes, homemade saps, other tools of a sordid trade. And he knew their restless needs would not be sated until they basked in the sounds of breaking bone and whimpered pleas for mercy.

Forrester closed his eyes and breathed deeply; none of my affair, he thought. I have other work to do, important work. God's work. And as soon as those infernal ruffians move on, I'll be at it.

A moment passed, and another, as the sound of shuffling boots receded. Then Forrester stepped from the alley, oiled cogs at his knees and elbows rotating smoothly, a soft puff of steam venting from the iron and brass apparatus he wore on his back. He looked left, satisfied that the miscreant gang had rounded a corner and was no longer in sight, then began walking in the other direction.

Until a new sound broke the silence of the nearly deserted,

night-shrouded streets: a scream, forlorn and frightened. Female.

Forrester hesitated. He had a calling, and no time to lose. Any delay could mean the difference between justice and transgression, life and death. But then a ghost of memory slipped through his thoughts: another time, another scream. His head tilted, looking back the way he'd come.

***

"Why, Lady Catherine. I wasn't aware you had an interest in science."

The university amphitheatre buzzed softly with the sound of low conversation as spectators found their seats. And William Forrester smiled with genuine pleasure as Catherine Meadows took a place beside him in the front row.

"I'm interested in anything that might promote a better life, m'lord," Catherine responded with a smile of her own. "Especially for those whose lives are limited by their station."

On a raised platform before them, Professor Lawrence Kesslemeade moved with sharp, birdlike motions, puttering around banks of esoteric paraphernalia, checking dials and adjusting switches. A mousy woman in a starched lab coat followed him, taking notes, stealing nervous glances at the growing audience. It was obvious she was more comfortable in a laboratory than on a stage.

"Ever the reformer, eh, m'lady?" Forrester chided, then leaned closer and whispered conspiratorially, "But you might be wise to keep your progressive notions under your bonnet. The Queen, may God keep her, has ears everywhere."

Lady Catherine's smile thinned as she turned her head back to the stage. "And does she own yours as well, m'lord? You've always seemed so comfortable in your cloak of wealth and prestige, caring nought for those who weren't born to your advantages. I would think that a man of your position wouldn't need another thirty pieces of silver."

Forrester's eyes took in the woman's profile, her straw-colored hair and alabaster skin, and thought, not for the first time, that their children would be beautiful.

"There's something to be said for order, Catherine: everything—and everyone—in its place. But as for silver, I put a great

deal more than thirty pieces into funding the good professor's research. Let us hope it was worth the show he's about to give us."

***

"C'mon, girlie, give us a kiss, eh?"

The leering hooligan pressed his bulk against the young woman, pinning her to the abandoned storefront, his breath stinking of cheap ale and rotting teeth. The frightened girl struggled to pull away, lips quivering as she spoke.

"P-Please! I just...m-my mother! She needs medicine! I-I was—"

"Don't fret, darlin'," the thug cooed a gravely purr. "Yer mum'll have it a lot easier with one less mouth ta feed!"

The other ruffians chortled and pushed, gathering closer, eager for their turn. When a new voice sounded from behind, cold and hard as January ice.

"Let her go...and I'll let you live."

As one the bullyboys whirled, hands reaching for lead pipes and ugly knives.

"Copper!"

But the figure that stepped from the emerald-tinted fog was something more: over six feet tall, clad entirely in deep crimson, filagreed metal gauntlets shrouding each hand. A network of wires and thin tubes connected those gauntlets to a softly puffing backpack, and to disclike cogs at elbows and knees. A leather hood covered his head, masking all expression, but the menace in his stance was clear even to the thick-headed hoodlums.

"Gor'! I-It's 'im! The Righteous Red!"

"But that's just a tale fer scarin' the li'l ones!"

"Feh!" The gang's leader stepped forward, mouth drooping in a snarl as he slipped a rusty cleaver from his belt. "Fairy story or not, these streets are ours! I say we see how red he is on the inside!"

***

Professor Kesslemeade stepped to the front of the raised platform, cleared his throat, and spoke in an academic baritone that carried throughout the large hall.

"The prospectus that was included with your invitations gave the background of what I am about to demonstrate. But for those who hadn't the time to read it, or have someone read it for them..." The timid woman in the lab coat fought to suppress a grin. "...allow me to summarize."

Turning to a central table, the Professor draped his hand over a black stone approximately a meter in diameter, covered in jagged pocks, connected by wires and clamps to a surrounding series of esoteric machinery.

"This rock was found in a deep crevice by engineers clearing a quarry on the edge of Oak Heath. It maintained an oddly persistent warmth, and seemed to evidence pulsations from the interior. The foreman who brought it to me speculated that it may have been thrust to the surface by the same disruption that created Fulbright's crater. We may never know. But what my examination and experiments suggest is that it may well house a heretofore unknown form of energy. One that I believe has the potential to dwarf the power of electromagnetism and steam combined!"

Gasps of astonishment hissed through the auditorium. A bearded man in the third row stood and pointed an angry finger at the professor.

"Do you take us for fools, sir? Do you actually expect us to believe—"

Kesslemeade raised a hand to silence the man. "I expect you to believe nothing. Nothing but what your eyes will soon show you."

The Professor indicated an iron safe next to the center table, a waist-high box of the type used by small business concerns to store payrolls and such. "This vault weighs over a hundred kilograms. But by merely coursing energy from the black rock through its mass, it will be lifted into the air to a point roughly level with my head."

Gasps gave way to cries, as shouts of "Impossible!" and "Madness!" accompanied Kesslemeade to a control panel. Knobs were turned, keys depressed, and a deep thrum began to grow as the black stone became bathed in a wavering blue aura. William Forrester felt the floor vibrate beneath the soles of his day boots.

While behind the Professor, his assistant's eyes grew wide, and she took an uneasy step back from the table. Which is when two unforeseen things occurred: the iron safe suddenly jerked and rose, tumbling like a leaf in autumn wind, one sharp corner striking the frightened woman. Who in turn barked a startled scream and staggered sideways, colliding with one of the banks of machinery. Wires tore loose, blasting a burst of sparks into the air.

Streaks of blue lightning shot from the black stone, splitting and twisting, piercing walls and windows, filling the hall with breaking glass and the rumble of imminent disaster.

Rising from his seat, eyes locked on the erupting chaos before him, Forrester said simply:

"Catherine. Run!"

***

The leader lunged, and William Forrester cocked an arm, curling fingers into a fist. One of those fingers pressed an indentation in the palm of his gauntlet and the fist pistoned forward like a cannon shot. Knuckles met nose in a crack of ruined cartilage, snapping the leader's head back, fountaining blood. The young man's feet slid forward, kicking high, and his back struck the cobbled pavement with a meaty thud.

But a second tough was already crouching low, and sent a butcher's blade slicing under Forrester's arm, eliciting a grunt of pain. But before he could strike a second time, he was seized by the throat and lifted off his feet. Forrester's backpack wheezed louder as he swung the churl in a lightning-swift arc, slamming him with dramatic force into a nearby lamp post. The ruffian slid, broken and slack, to the blood-streaked cobbles.

While yet a third rowdy sprang from behind, wielding a sharpened chisel. But Forrester spun at the waist, faster than humanly possible, grasped the young man's wrist before a blow could be struck. "You should have learned from your friends' mistakes." A popping hiss built slowly as blue sparks formed along the intricate filigree of Forrester's gauntlet. "Now you've made your own."

Azure flame sizzled and flashed up the thug's arm, and a startled cry was cut short as fire erupted around his head. Once-brown eyes simmered and blackened, and he dropped to the pavement in an unmoving heap.

The remaining Mourning Lads, evidencing a slow but eventual wisdom, sprinted off in random directions.

***

Walls shook, and debris rained from a cracking ceiling as spectators fled to the auditorium's exit doors. Forrester followed that mad rush for survival, urging Catherine up the stairs before him. As she passed through one of the waiting portals, a thin cry cut through the mingled shouts of panic and prayer. Forrester stopped and turned, and through the growing haze of smoke and tumbling detritus saw Kesslemeade's assistant still on the stage. She was lying on her side; a heavy machine had fallen, pinning her foot. Eyes wide with terror, she reached a hand out to him, mouth forming desperate words that were lost in the shattering roar that filled the hall.

Forrester hesitated. Chivalry demanded that he go to her aid. Yet practicality spoke with equal firmness: this was her fault, after all. She was obviously lowborn, and clumsy at that. Could her life possibly be worth his own? Heartbeats passed, alternatives were hastily considered, until at last a decision was made. William Forrester took a step—

—and his world turned blue...then white...then...

Black.

***

Forrester approached the young woman, who trembled slightly as she smoothed her bodice, watching him in wide-eyed wonder.

"You...you're really him? The Righteous Red?"

"I've been called that, among other things."

He bent to retrieve a paper-wrapped bundle the woman had dropped, handed it to her as she continued.

"Father Cody talked about you in his sermon. Said you claimed to be God's hand, but that what you did was more like..." She lowered her gaze. "...the devil."

"God works in mysterious ways. I know that more truly than most." He slipped a gold watch from inside his frock coat, shoulders sagging slightly as he read the dial.

The woman looked up again. "But why? Why do this at all?"

Forrester snapped an answer with thinning patience. "Your peril has cost me much already, young woman. Do you expect me to waste more time justifying my actions?" He then added as he turned to walk into the fog, "Go home. Salvation is an inconstant friend, and might not find you a second time."

***

Moments later, in the shadowed doorway of a derelict tenement, Forrester pressed a stud on his backpack, sending an electric burst on a specific wavelength. Soon after, a midnight blue steam coach slowed to a halt, a rear door opened and, assuring himself that he was unobserved, Forrester slid quickly inside.

At the wheel, a compact man with thinning ginger hair turned and inquired, "Are you all right, m'lord? You seem to be favoring your left side."

"That's none of your concern, Jenkins. Take me to the Trust; I've things to do."

The small man turned back to the wheel. "As you wish, m'lord."

Permitting himself to relax at last, Forrester leaned back against plush cushions and slipped the leather hood from his head, revealing the face of a man of thirty-five years, brown hair sweat-slicked on a high brow over an aquiline nose and troubled violet eyes. He allowed those eyes to slowly close as, with the ease of familiarity, Jenkins turned a dial, slid a lever, and the private coach pulled smoothly from the kerb.

***

Shortly thereafter, the softly chugging vehicle rolled down Chalk Street, an area of small shops and middle class residences. A Queen's Regulator stood watch on a corner, his pistol and billy club assuring citizens that they were safe from the likes of the Mourning Lads. Whether they would be safe from the Regulator himself was something discussed only in whispers.

In the middle of the block, the coach slowed and turned into a narrow passageway next to a building that sported a modest gilt-on-teak sign: "The Pemberton Trust", with smaller letters below reading, "Societal Adjustments Facilitated." At the end of the alley, Forrester—now clothed in fashionable great coat, vest and trousers, his crimson garb and accouterments carried in a closed wicker basket—stepped from the coach and inserted a key into the lock of an unmarked door, closing it behind him as he stepped inside.

The private office was spacious, furnished tastefully but without pretension: comfortable chairs, a polished mahogany desk, walls adorned with simple woodcuts and scenic prints. The clients he saw here were often hesitant, and he made every effort to reduce the natural intimidation of addressing someone obviously above their station. After making certain the door to the inner rooms was bolted, Forrester crossed to a far wall where a decorative mosaic plaque was mounted beside a bookcase. He pushed pieces of colored stone in a specific order, and the bookcase slid sideways to reveal a smaller, hidden chamber beyond.

Entering the secret room, Forrester put the wicker basket down and sat before a washstand and mirror. He poured water from a porcelain pitcher into a large bowl, then began to carefully remove coat, cravat and shirt. As he disrobed, his gaze moved idly around the gaslit chamber, glancing over shelves that displayed an eclectic array of mechanical gadgets, weapons, and implements of curious design. His eyes slowed only when they found an item that seemed oddly out of place: a woman's shoe, its coarse leather tattered and singed. Contrasted next to it was a book bound in the softest suede, edges worn smooth from time and use. He ran a finger down the Bible's spine.

"How long, God? And how many? Will it ever be enough...?"

He waited for an answer, and when none came, turned back to the washstand, dipped a cloth in water, and began to clean the shallow seeping wound in his side.

***

Morning came to New Southampton, slowly and incomplete. Sunlight that fought daily to push through the perpetual verdant haze cloaking the city succeeded only partially, providing illumination but little warmth.

At the palace of Queen Anne Eliza Wintersmith, the pomp and bustle of courtly activity was well under way. In the throne room, the Queen herself sat in regal posture, giving audience to the day's early supplicants—merchants and lesser dignitaries seeking favor: a tax exemption for luxury imports, a royal pardon for a relative's minor violation. The Queen's frown showed frail tolerance for these necessary but tedious proceedings, and hid little of her contempt for the treacly words and false smiles of the askers.

While outside, in a rear courtyard, darker business was being conducted. Roderick Gaunt, Captain of the Queen's personal guard, held watch over a convoy of steam carts entering through an opened gate. Little escaped the sweep of the Captain's slate-gray eyes as he stood erect, arms clasped hand-to-wrist behind his back, the grim line of his scowl deepening a comma-shaped scar on his chin. So far, he thought, so good.

A hand-picked squad of Regulators rimmed the courtyard, all leather and buckles, pistols and hard stares. Unusual security for a mere delivery procedure, but as Captain Gaunt and few others knew, there was nothing *mere* about this morning's shipment.

A creak and thump caught the Captain's ear as the last cart's wheel struck a jutting imperfection in the paving stones, forcing the vehicle's flat bed to rise. The cart's cargo, a wooden crate sealed with lock and chain, slid toward the edge.

Gaunt reacted with immediate command: "Secure that crate, you sluggards! If it hits the ground, your heads will keep it company!"

Two Regulators rushed to the cart, reaching it as the crate began to tip over the side. Straining against the obvious weight, they were just able to shoulder the crate back onto the bed as the cart inched ahead onto smoother pavement.

Gaunt's fisted knuckles stretched white as he strode forward, a scathing rebuke ready for the careless driver—when a voice as melodious as birdsong stopped him.

"Oh, my. Such masterful authority truly sets my heart a-flutter!"

The Captain stopped and turned, recognition softening his expression as he saw a young woman standing in the still-open gateway.

"Why, Lady Catherine. What a delightful surprise."

With a rustle of silk, an open if unneeded parasol resting on her shoulder, Catherine Meadows took two steps into the courtyard. Captain Gaunt hurried to block her way, offering a small bow of apology.

"Please, m'lady, you can't be here. I realize you're welcome in the palace—Queen Anne finds your attitudes on class equality quite amusing—but this area is currently forbidden to all but sanctioned personnel."

"Really?" Catherine replied in round-eyed innocence as she took in the ranks of grim-faced Regulators. "All this for a delivery of victuals? Oh, I do hope there's more of those little pomegranate pastries. They simply *made* the Queen's last gala! That is, until the...incident."

"Ah, yes," the Captain answered with a frown of remembrance. "The rabble with their stones and signs, whining about this and that. But don't worry..." Gaunt turned his head to where workers were carrying cargo from the steam carts into an open door—not noticing how Catherine's gaze subtly followed his own. "...such interruptions will soon be a thing of the past. I guarantee it."

Then, returning his attention to the young woman, "Now, please, you must go. You wouldn't want me to suffer the Queen's anger...?"

Catherine lowered her head in compliance. "Of course not, Captain. I understand completely."

She turned and began to walk back to the gate, where Regulators stood at each side waiting to close the heavy oaken doors. Gaunt cleared his throat and addressed the departing woman. "It was a pleasure speaking with you, m'lady. Will I...see you again?"

Catherine slowed her walk. "Anything is possible..." Then turned her head to glance back with a playful grin. "...Roderick."

Gaunt watched as Lady Catherine strolled through the gate, his lungs filling with what he would never admit was a sigh. Then pivoted and walked back into the courtyard as the massive gate doors creaked shut. Thus he failed to see Catherine Meadows stop before a hunched beggar in the street outside. Failed to see her drop a coin into the man's bowl. Failed to hear her whisper, "This entrance. Midnight. Bring the others."

He would live to regret that oversight.

***

"Really, William, I do wish you'd show more respect for my

inventions. At least clean the bloody things once in a while!"

Lawrence Kesslemeade stood at a table scattered with Righteous Red paraphernalia, oiling a cog here, scraping a valve there. Gaslight flickered over the stone walls of the low-ceilinged room, originally a wine cellar at The Falls, country estate of the Lords Pemberton for many generations, now cluttered with an exhaustive array of complex and experimental scientific apparatus.

At one side of the room, William Forrester paced back and forth, hands behind his back, brow furrowed with barely contained forbearance.

"You're paid well for your contraptions, Professor, and for your time."

"Yes, that's true," the scientist mumbled as he removed a small glass-tipped cylinder from an open panel in the backpack. "But I can't help wondering what would happen were I to introduce this conversion module to the world at large. Rather brilliant, I must say, how it expands steam violently, allowing a tiny amount to exert tremendous pressure. That's what lets your arms and legs to act as steam pistons, you know, multiplying your native strength."

"I'm well aware of that, Professor. It's saved my life more than once."

"But imagine the revolution in manufacturing, in technology, imagine the fame and fortune—! Why, if the world knew of this amazing breakthrough—"

"The Queen would steal it and you'd lie rotting in an unmarked grave."

Kesslemeade cleared his throat, carefully replacing the cylinder in its backpack cradle. "Well...there is that."

Then, resting his hands on the table surface as a wistful smile lifted the corners of his mouth, "Still, such advances would be a fitting tribute to poor Martha. So sad. All that was left was a shoe."

Forrester slowed his pacing, then stopped to lower himself onto a padded bench. "A regrettable loss," he responded in tones of dubious conviction, "but unavoidable. An act of fate."

"Perhaps." Kesslemeade spoke softly as he returned to his maintenance chores. "But it was certainly a different fate that smiled upon you, William, keeping you farther from the eruption. You were the lucky one."

Forrester leaned his head back against the wall, eyes focusing inward.

"An interesting perspective, Professor. 'The lucky one...'"

***

The black world had turned white again, but this time it was the white of clean linen and scrubbed hospital walls. Three days had passed. Private surgeons had declared Lord Pemberton's condition miraculous, marveling at how his body had only suffered minor burns similar to heat exposure, while his heavy clothing had been reduced to ash. Ultimately, there'd been nothing they could do but release him to return to The Falls after a further day's observation.

And it had been at that family refuge that William Forrester had soon discovered his survival had not been the only surprising result of the black stone's violent detonation. He'd been sitting in the library when Rex, the hulking mastiff that had been his loyal companion for years, padded into the room. But instead of crossing to his master's side, the great animal had stopped short, growling, lips pulled back over dripping fangs. Forrester's anger, never far from the surface since his awakening, burst forth as he reached for the dog, shouting in reprimand. Only to stop, stunned, as blue sparks crackled along his arm, and sizzling cerulean fire shot from his hand to envelop the loyal Rex, incinerating the howling hound in a stench of smoldering fur and boiling blood.

Forrester had risen in horror, heart racing as streaks of cobalt flame sprang from his fingers, shoulders, eyes, growing in intensity as panic increased. Books burned, glass shattered, screams raged—his screams—until at last darkness had returned, this time a welcome escape.

It had been luck alone that Jenkins, Forrester's longtime personal servant, had entered the library in time to see the last blue flickers as his lord and master collapsed to the floor. But it had been awareness and acumen that had led Jenkins to contact Professor Kesslemeade, rather than local emergency services.

In the days that followed, tests had been performed, an hypothesis proposed: Kesslemeade suggested that William Forrester's body might have absorbed the unknown energy emitted by the black stone when it shattered. Energy that could now be released—

or contained—by Forrester's will. And so a laboratory had been equipped in the unused wine cellar, where further experiments confirmed Kesslemeade's speculation. But while a reasonable "what" had been determined, a more perplexing question remained: "why?"

***

"You didn't actually kill her, you know."

Forrester rose at Kesslemeade's comment, restless once more, and resumed pacing as he spoke.

"The time I could have used to save her was spent in questioning, in hesitance. She was common, yes, but she was one of God's creatures, and I let her die. My condition, this...curse, is God's punishment. It must be. And I can only pray that if I show proper contrition, if I counter enough sin to make up for my weakness, He will forgive me. And in His mercy, allow me once more to become... human."

Kesslemeade snapped a last clasp and set the heavy steampack upright on the table. "Well, whatever the reason, you're making a difference in people's lives. And that in itself is—"

"Yes, yes," Forrester waved an impatient hand. "Are you quite done? That silly woman with her mother's medicine caused me to miss the rendezvous last night. And if the rumors Vole passed along, about some secret material being unloaded at the Queen's landing, something that could cost hundreds of lives, are true..."

"Understood." Kesslemeade lowered the backpack into the wicker basket that already held Forrester's crimson leathers. "The Righteous Red needs to be prepared!"

***

Roderick Gaunt grinned, his facial muscles almost straightening the comma-shaped scar on his chin. The work was going well.

The bulk of the warehouse in which he stood had been cleared, the crates delivered on steam carts that morning now empty and pushed aside with unused furniture, statuary and other miscellany. While in the open center, technicians went about assembling the contents of those crates: strange wired components were clipped into waiting sockets, iron castings were riveted together, alloy antennae were screwed into finely milled nodes. The clack and slam of hammers and other tools echoed through the high-ceilinged chamber as three large and ominous forms began to take shape.

Captain Gaunt removed a uniform glove and ran appreciative fingers along the cold gray side of one of the mechanisms. Its elements had been manufactured on his personal recommendation, and he was certain a knighthood would follow once their value had been demonstrated. His thoughts strayed to that future advancement as his hand slid idly over an angled opening rimmed with rows of wedge-shaped metal—until he jerked the hand back with a sharp grunt of pain. Blood dripped from his fingers.

His grin grew to a smile.

***

“Lord Pemberton?” Agatha Mumford poked her head around the door to William Forrester’s office with an expression of tolerant distaste. “I apologize for the intrusion, sir, but there’s a...ahem...person here who insists on seeing you. A Mister Vole.”

Forrester sat up straighter behind his desk, looking past a plain, middle-aged woman seated on the other side. “Thank you, Miss Mumford. Tell him I’ll be but a moment.”

Hurriedly, Forrester stood and offered a hand to his somewhat puzzled client, encouraging her to rise as he rounded the desk. “You may ease your worries, Mrs. Thornton. You have my personal assurance that you and your husband will not be routed from your home.”

So much busywork, he thought as he showed the woman out. He’d started this charitable trust as a way to gain information on great evils that needed to be confronted. But dealing with such petty problems as unfair evictions was an irritation necessary to keep up appearances. He’d buy the hovel where this sad woman lived, lower her rent, then evict the greedy landlord. Not exactly saving the world, but a small correction God might notice.

Forrester was back at his desk a moment later when a short, bat-faced man in rough clothing entered, dragging an unpleasant air of ancient sweat with him. He approached the desk with hat in hands, mouth sporting a jaunty yellow grin.

“Got yer message, squire. Sorry ta hear yer agent missed that transfer at the landin’ last night.”

“Your concern is touching, Vole. And useless. Have you anything of *value* to offer?”

“Well, now,” Vole mused as his fingers tickled the brim of his bowler. “I weren’t able to suss exactly what was in that shipment, but I did ferret out where it got took. ‘Course, with the amount o’ danger to me own person involved...” his eyes narrowed, “...I figger I should get bigger pay.”

Forrester said nothing, simply glared unblinking at the man before him.

And while Vole didn’t know the precise word for what he saw in that gaze, he understood on a feral level that it was the mirror opposite of “mercy.” His grin faded.

“Then again, seein’ as how we’re pals an’ all, I-I reckon the usual’d be just fine.”

Forrester opened a drawer, removed a cloth pouch jangling with metal coins. Vole stared at the purse with open greed.

“Storeroom inside the southwest gate o’ the Queen’s palace. The big one, on the left side. Um, yer lordship.”

Vole caught the purse as it was tossed, jerked a nervous nod and left the office. While Forrester, leaning forward in his chair, drummed fingers on the desk top, a tense anticipatory rhythm. This could be big, he thought. But... big enough? He lowered his head in silent prayer.

***

Streetlamps battled fog and darkness as night fell once more over New Southampton. Darkness won, and William Forrester, The Righteous Red, made his way unseen to the twelve-foot wall surrounding a rear courtyard of Queen Ann’s palace. Midnight was near, and he knew this was the hour when shifts changed, when current guards would be weary, their senses dulled. And indeed, no one heard as Forrester crouched, as compressed steam sprang his legs straight again and lofted him to the top of the imposing wall.

He adjusted the goggles Professor Kesslemeade had provided. Their multiple lenses gathered even the smallest available light, allowing him to see as if it were merely dusk. The courtyard was empty. Good, he thought, that should simplify—

Chnk! Khk! Chak!

Forrester snapped his head left, to where the wall he was on mated flush with the top of a windowless outbuilding. His hearing, slightly enhanced by the alien energy coursing through him, had caught the sound of three grapples, prongs muted by wrapped cloth, digging into the low rim of that building's edge. As he watched, a dozen men clambered over onto the roof, clubs and other improvised weapons in belts or slung on backs. Their leader—shorter than the rest, his head covered pirate-style in a wound bandana cut with eye-holes—immediately set them to opening one of two skylights meant to let in weak sunrays during daylight hours.

As he made his way along the top of the wall, Forrester saw that one man carried a keg marked with a triple "x": black powder. He shook his head: why, God? Why curse me further with well-meaning idiots? He didn't even try to mask his arrival as he stepped to the roof, the crunch of cinders under his boots causing the invaders to whirl and draw their weapons. He held out a hand, palm forward.

"I've no wish to fight you. And unless you're even bigger fools than you appear, you've no wish to fight me."

The diminutive leader stepped forward, brandishing a small caliber pistol. For a lowborn to possess such a weapon was a death sentence; Forrester wondered if this lad was simply brave, or...

"We've a job to do, Mister...Red, is it? You can help us, you can leave...or you can die."

Forrester stopped cold, his hidden face frozen in shock. Not at the words, but at the voice that had spoken them. The loose clothing could disguise familiar curves, the wrapped bandana hide straw-coloured hair. But that voice, and the lips that formed it...

Catherine?

Mistaking his hesitation for acquiescence, the trespassers began to lower themselves down the grapple ropes, now dangling from the open skylight. As Catherine joined them, Forrester regained his composure and leaped through the opening himself, his backpack hissing as it fed force into the tubes along his legs, gentling the impact as he landed on the hard floor twenty feet below.

"M'lady," Forrester began as he strode forward into the gloomy gaslit expanse, his lowered voice further muffled by the leather of his hood. Catherine cocked her head in response, puzzling at the title of respect.

"This is no place for a person of breeding. Such muckwork should be left to—"

"To whom?" Catherine snapped back. "The authorities who crush every effort the common man makes to better his lot? The aristocracy who turn their heads on injustice so long as it doesn't effect their social schedule? Do you realize there are highborns who've had servants for decades, but don't even know their Christian names? Yet asked the name of their dog or prize stallion and it's on the tip of their tongue! Leave the future of thousands to *them*?"

Catherine's words stung, in some way he didn't quite understand. Still, he reached a gauntleted hand for her arm.

"This isn't the time for discussion. You're leaving."

Catherine's companions began to close around them, weapons held tightly. When a new voice sounded from behind.

"Oh, do stay. I insist!"

All eyes turned to see Roderick Gaunt step from around a stack of crates. A rectangular box hung from a strap around his neck, lying flat at his waist like the tray of a beggar selling poppies on the street. But this box sported instead an array of slide switches and knurled knobs. Gaunt continued to speak as the intruders moved warily back, taking defensive positions.

"I'd rather hoped for such an opportunity. With acts of social disruption on the rise, I thought it likely someone might get wind of this operation. And now you've provided the perfect test for my new friends."

So saying, Gaunt flipped a toggle on the control panel before him. At Catherine's side, one of her followers bent at the waist, crying out as he covered both ears with his hands.

"Sonics," Gaunt explained. "Too shrill for all but the most sensitive to hear, designed to transmit to coordinated receivers. The original purpose was to aid the military, protect our homeland from invasion. But then I realised how helpful such technology could be in controlling certain elements *within* that homeland."

A sound of grinding gears drew all eyes to the surrounding shadows, from which a trio of grotesqueries clanked forward on cog-kneed limbs. Roughly resembling dogs, or wolves, they were the size of African elephants. Their eyes blazed yellow, like fist-sized suns, and razored triangles of teeth lined their rhythmically snapping jaws.

"Now let me see..." Gaunt's hand hovered over the controls, "...what was the frequency for—" then lowered to move a slide switch forward. "—ah, yes.

"Kill!"

The clockwork monsters sprang forward, and Catherine Meadows reacted instantly, raising her revolver to fire three quick shots. But while the bullets struck true, they had no more effect than pebbles thrown at a mountain. And it was only Forrester's energy-enhanced speed that allowed him to push her out of the way, tumbling them both into a pile of excelsior as the lead dog pounced, metal claws gouging grooves in the stone where they'd stood mere heartbeats before.

Screams and shouts raked the air as Forrester helped Catherine to her feet. Across the room, one of her men was being disemboweled by a second giant dog. She grabbed Forrester's arm: "Help them!"

"Of course, m'lady. As soon as I've gotten you away and—"

"They're being slaughtered *now*! Help them, for God's sake!"

Truth, blazing in the intensity of pale eyes behind a bandana mask, made the decision for him. "Yes. For God's sake."

Thus the Righteous Red crouched, and a steam-powered leap took him to land behind the second monstrous dog, who continued to bat at the now lifeless form of its recent victim. A stack of granite blocks was stored nearby, likely meant for future repairs to the palace. Forrester's backpack hissed as it directed force to help him lift one of the ponderous slabs, and the sound brought the dog's head around in a silent snarl. But as it lunged to attack, Forrester slammed the granite block forward, leaning into the blow, smashing the quarried stone into the clockwork creature's muzzle with a crash like muted thunder. Metal shards scattered as the massive hound staggered backwards. But before Forrester could follow through with a killing blow, he heard new cries; two more of Catherine's followers were being menaced by the third dog. He turned and ran in that direction.

While at the opposite end of the warehouse, Roderick Gaunt

glared in anger. "This will *not* do!" He concentrated on the control board at his waist, twisted a dial. "But raising the aggression imperative to maximum should—*AGK!*"

The startled Captain pitched forward onto the floor, following the impact of the broken table leg that had impacted his shoulders. As he struggled to rise, the same beam smashed down on the control board that had slipped from his neck. He looked up in surprise to see the rebels' slender leader holding that makeshift cudgel.

"You've stopped nothing, bumpkin! Without further input, the beasts will simply follow their last command! The order to—"

An approaching whir of gyroscopic gears brought Gaunt's head around. The first of the clockwork horrors was stalking towards them, jaws opening and closing on rows of finely filed fangs.

"...kill?"

Across the cavernous room, William Forrester neared a scene of butchery. One of the two insurgents lay in wet pieces, while the other had been backed into a corner, barely keeping the monstrous hound at bay with a stubby 2X4. But rather than slow his pace, Forrester's steam-pistoned legs pumped even faster, slamming him into the giant predator's haunch, knocking it onto its side with a reverberant clang. It lay struggling to rise, legs peddling like some freakish terrapin flipped on its back.

The rescued rebel smiled through a trickle of blood from a head wound, held his hand out to The Righteous Red. "I know our lady weren't too happy ya showed up, mate, but I'm damned glad ya did! Name's Timothy—put 'er there."

But before Forrester could decide whether to take the proffered hand, Timothy's eyes widened, looking past his crimson-clad savior. "Oh, no! M'lady—!"

Forrester turned as Timothy sprinted past him, saw the cause of the young man's fear: Catherine and the Queen's Guard were being herded against a wall by another of the metallic wolf-dogs! He started to follow, hoping compressed steam fed to the connections on his legs would get him to the threatened couple before—*whoof!*

Something struck from behind, knocking Forrester to the ground, pushing the breath from his lungs. The hound he'd bashed with the granite slab had him pinned with a front paw the size of a carriage wheel. It's lower jaw was crumpled and unmoving, but the beast seemed determined to take his head anyway. Its remaining razored teeth swung closer...closer.

While at the other side of the room, Roderick Gaunt drew his pistol, knowing it was futile gesture. Beside him, the dissident leader stood steadfast, the table leg in a tight grip. Plucky lad, Gaunt thought. If I have to die, it could be in worse company.

But then a cry of defiance cut through the ongoing din of battle, as Timothy flung himself from a stack of crates to land on the stalking wolf-dog's back. The mechanical brute immediately bolted, determined to throw its rider, a struggle that ended quickly when the bucking beast jerked shoulders forward, slinging its uninvited passenger into a wall with a slap of bruising flesh.

While across the spacious chamber, William Forrester planted his palms flat on the floor, pistoning his arms to thrust himself upward. The metal paw slipped from his back and he whirled, reaching to grab the giant dog's dislocated mandible. With a screeching twist he wrenched the jaw loose, sending the mangled creature tumbling to one side. Without hesitation, Forrester turned and dashed off.

Staggering to his feet, Timothy fought to breathe, his mouth bubbling blood from a punctured lung. Through fading vision he saw Catherine in danger once more, but now he saw something else: the keg of black powder that had been dropped when the attack had begun. He lifted it in his arms, lurched toward the stalking metal hound. "Hey...Rover! Whyn't ya...snack on...me first!"

As if angered by yet another interruption, the dog whipped around and snatched Timothy in its jaws, lifting him into the air as gears tightened, bones cracked.

Forrester slowed as he neared the massive beast, saw Timothy dangling from its iron maw, still clutching the powder keg. The battered man's voice whispered through blooded teeth: "Save 'er...mate." Adding, as Forrester seemed to hesitate, "Back's broke...I'm through. Do...what ya gotta."

And so, eyes narrowing in concentration behind his hood, Forrester raised both gauntlets. Blue sparks began to spit and jump along their filagree, building, expanding, until a blanket of azure flame covered his arms hand-to-elbow. He then pistoned those arms forward, and bolts of blue fire shot from his fists, striking the dying rebel—and the keg of black powder he held. The explosion shook ceiling and walls, knocking Catherine Meadows and Roderick Gaunt off their feet, scattering gobbets of flesh and skitters of twisted metal through the air as the now-headless dog tilted, then collapsed to the floor.

Ignoring the barely conscious Gaunt, Forrester rushed to help Catherine stand as new noise intruded: Regulators from within the palace, drawn by the sound of the detonation, had begun pounding on the barred door to the warehouse.

"Are you hurt?" Forrester asked.

"Not *yet*," the young woman replied, pointing over his shoulder.

Forrester turned to see the remaining two dog-things, one snapping its still-intact jaws, slinking slowly towards them, side-by-side, as if confident of an easy victory.

"Enough," Forrester said simply as he began to walk, then trot, then sprint on a collision course with the approaching beasts. But just before reaching them, he dove under their pivoting heads in a tuck roll, came to one knee between them and shot his arms laterally, Kesslemeade's conversion module giving him strength to dig fingers deep into the metal monsters' sides. As they fought to pull free, Forrester focused his will, and a deep blue aura began to dance around him. Flicker became flame, brightened, then pulsed and spread, slithering up his arms onto the metal hides of the canine abominations. Soon, all three were bathed in a wash of searing cobalt fire. Clockwork creations feel no pain, but the desperation in their mad efforts to pull free showed some innate sense of self-preservation. Though in the end their efforts fell short, as the man-made monsters puddled to the floor, limbs softening, bodies melting into twin heaps of smoldering gray slag. It was only then that William Forrester released his grip, allowing the fading blue energy to flow back into his body.

The tick and ping of cooling metal joined the sound of renewed pounding on the warehouse door as Forrester held a hand out to Catherine: "They'll be through soon. We have to go."

Catherine looked to where her three remaining followers, wounded and bleeding, struggled to climb the dangling grapple ropes. "My friends—!"

"Have shown their mettle. They'll live. Now come, m'lady." Forrester wrapped an arm around Catherine's waist, crouched and sprang in a perfect arc that took them through the skylight to the roof.

While behind them, only now beginning to regain his senses, Roderick Gaunt rose to one elbow and whispered, “M...m’lady...?”

***

Catherine Meadows and William Forrester stood on a flat rooftop, watching through emerald mist as smoke and chaos rose from the Queen’s palace some streets away. There was silence between them, until Forrester spoke in a satisfied tone: “Theirs was a costly failure, unlikely to be repeated. You should be pleased.”

Catherine slipped the bandana from her head as she turned, ringlets of damp yellow hair curling over her ears.

“Pleased? Nine good men died tonight! Timothy alone had a wife, two sons. Should I drop by their flat and inform *them* how pleased they should be?”

“Victory always has cost, m’lady. Be grateful it was pennies tonight, instead of pounds.”

Catherine’s mouth dropped open, then snapped shut in a tight line, the light in her blue eyes flaring nearly as bright as the cerulean fire that had earlier crackled from Forrester’s fists.

“Pennies?! Because they were lowborn? You talk like an educated man, but there's ignorance between your words. You claim to care, to be Heaven’s hand, yet you judge others by circumstance rather than by their souls!”

“*God* made the world, m’lady, not I. If He’d wanted all men to be equal they would be. Those who deserve privilege are born to it. Others are set on Earth to provide for the more worthy. It is God’s will.”

“Really?” Catherine stared up into the shadowed eyeholes of Forrester’s hood. “Then perhaps you should reread your bible, Mr. Righteous Red. You seem to have forgotten one small thing: God’s own son was a carpenter!”

She turned and walked through the fog toward a descending stairway, her voice growing as distant as her manner.

“Do your work for God, then—I’ll do mine for the rest of us.”

***

Then next morning brought rain to New Southampton, a constant dirty drizzle like ash-gray tears. In the ground floor library at The Falls, William Forrester sat in a high-backed chair, chin on fist, watching wet rivulets glide down panes of leaded glass. He'd been there since dawn, rarely moving, saying nothing.

A soft knock sounded, and Jenkins opened the library door to set foot a short distance inside.

"Pardon the intrusion, m'lord, but cook wants to know if you'd like your breakfast served here or in the conservatory?"

Jenkins waited patiently for several moments; then, receiving no answer, turned to leave. He'd been in Lord Pemberton's service long enough to recognize when the man was not to be disturbed. But as he started to close the door, he heard Forrester's voice speak softly.

"Jenkins?"

The attentive servant leaned his head back around the door. "Yes, m'lord?"

"What is your Christian name?"

Taken aback by the unprecedented familiarity, Jenkins could merely blink, unsure of what to say. "I...beg your pardon, m'lord?"

"You have a Christian name, don't you? Well, what is it?"

Increasingly uncomfortable with the nature of the conversation, Jenkins cleared his throat and stuttered. "It's, um, B-Bryan, sir. Bryan Jenkins."

Silence. And then, "Thank you, Jenkins. That will be all."

"Very good, m'lord." Clearly relieved, Jenkins turned and eased the library door shut behind him.

While in the high-backed chair, William Forrester continued to stare into the rain. Though in truth, he was looking at something far closer, far different. And far more troubling.

{*"Here is food for thought, but I do not like the thought it feeds."*}
Gerald Kersh
"The Brighton Monster"

CHARADA

by

Jennie Wood

The year was 2075, but that hardly mattered. I couldn't remember 2074 or 2073 or any year before. I couldn't remember anything earlier than three months ago, when I lay on an operating table in an underground base and was told my name was Riley. Staring at my reflection in the window of the steam-powered monorail, I tried to figure out who the hell I was.

My job was to capture defects, people who had the misfortune not to be like me, but I wanted to know more than my job. My hair was as short as the men I worked with. Hair as black as the clothes they gave us to wear and just long enough for a couple strands to escape from behind my ears and fall across my forehead. Black pants, black leather jacket, black knee high boots, black hooded shirt, even a black mechanical sleeve to fit over one arm. On the sleeve was a gun powered by a pump. The gun fired a dart that stunned the defects, knocking them out for a couple hours, more than enough time to get them back to base. To fire it, we pumped our fists. I did it, but I didn't understand it. I also didn't understand what made me different from a defect.

So many questions filled my mind. Like, why did we need sleeves if our arms and legs had been replaced with mechanical ones? Better weapons than the sleeve, our mechanical arms were strong enough to bust concrete, which we did in practice at the base, but our leaders told us we couldn't use the limbs to hurt the defects we captured. We were under strict orders not to harm, only to sedate them. We never saw our captures again after we dropped them off at the base infirmary. I had no idea who these captures were, what made them defects, what made them different from me.

Rumor around base was the doctors took their body parts, their organs to use on future recruits like me. Our new limbs were part steel, but also part bone and muscle and that had to come from somewhere. Odds were it came from the defects, but why? I also didn't know how we'd been recruited. The leaders made it sound like we'd had a choice, but the defects we kidnapped didn't have a choice.

The limb exchange did not compare to the number they did on our heads. We all had a small patch of missing hair in the back, a tender spot where they'd gone in. What they'd taken out or put in, none of us recruits knew. I didn't recognize this world nor did I remember any world before it. My hair was slowly growing to cover the spot in the back of my head, and I wondered: would I forget that too, once it was gone?

Goggles covered my grey eyes. They were required every time we went above ground due to Creeping Green, the mysterious moss colored smog that hovered over the entire city. I watched the smoke from the monorail disappear into Creeping Green. Word had it that Creeping Green caused a goggle-less guy on the street to go blind, then crazy. One of my fellow recruiters swore he'd seen it happen. Maybe it took our memories too. Maybe we'd all somehow been exposed to Creeping Green. My partners, Orion and Milo, couldn't remember anything before waking up at the base either.

Orion, Milo and I tightened our goggles, pulled up our hoods and filed off the monorail. We couldn't react to things like Creeping Green's musty stench, which greeted us every time we exited the train station. We were told to stick together and not to do anything to cause attention. We were dressed like all the other people walking around New Southampton. Soldiers and police had sleeves with guns similar to ours. Most people we passed on the street didn't look at us.

What bothered me most about these missions was the tugging feeling that it was wrong. We had to ID the defects by the numbers tattooed on the inside of their left arm. Everyone we picked up had a tattooed number. And they were never surprised to see us. Maybe they thought we were Transhumans or the United World Government (UWG), the two groups involved in an ongoing war so large it had been named The Great United World War. Our leaders assured us that we were neither Transhumans nor UWG, that we were an independent group, picking up evil defects. The defects didn't seem evil to me.

Like me, none of my comrades had tattooed numbers. Most of the people we picked up had darker skin than we did, especially darker than our leaders who were all blond hair and blue eyes. Our leaders' skin matched the porcelain tea sets used to serve morning tea. I asked our leaders about the tattooed numbers once over breakfast. They said the defects received the tattoos after losing a war a few years back and then they offered me more tea.

No one else questioned anything. Orion told me it was because they'd killed the last comrade who did. I asked Orion how the comrade was killed. He claimed not to know. It didn't make sense. We had mechanical limbs and our leaders did not. We could take them out. Thinking about it, my mouth grew dry, my stomach tightened. I fought off a growing urge to challenge them.

Orion, Milo and I exited the train station and passed the Red Lion Pub in a northern neighborhood of New Southampton. We followed the compass embedded in my sleeve and headed west toward the Solent Straight.

"Be nice to stop in, have a pint," Milo said.

"You know we cannot," Orion said.

We weren't allowed any excursions when we went above ground, and the only time we left the underground base was to pick up someone. Not that it mattered with the Red Lion, which was for members only. Who the members were exactly, I didn't know.

They resembled our leaders. Gas lamps burned in the windows and reflected light off their pale faces. Their blue eyes sparkled and their blond hair glowed as they crowded around tables.

As we walked by the door of the pub, I felt the warmth of its fireplace on my skin. The scents of cigars and fried foods made my mouth water. For a few seconds, I wanted to be one of the people inside. Then I reminded myself of my increasing suspicion that our leaders worked with these people. Perhaps these people wanted the defects out of their neighborhood.

New Southampton was the name of this district since it had been rebuilt after the great fire in 2030. The area we were now walking through had been rough back then, at the time of the fire, known for its alternative culture and music venues. Artists and musicians had lived there. I didn't remember any of this. Our leaders gave us a brief history and overview of the area since it's where we would be working.

My favorite part was a small park in the section where we usually picked up the defects. When the area was rebuilt they'd included the new park with a statue of Amy Winehouse, the legendary singer who died in the early part of the century. Our leaders had let us hear some of her music. Listening to her music was the only time since I woke up on the operating table that I'd found something familiar about this world. I'd heard her music, that voice before. It gave me hope that I'd remember more.

Larger gas lamps lit our way through the brick lined streets. Even with Creeping Green hovering above, the area was beautiful. The black iron over every window and door was designed to keep riff raff out, but still be pretty. The increased crime in the area wasn't going to get in the way of appearances in this section of New Southampton.

72 Thompson Street did not have the iron trimming or a gas lamp in the window. The house was rundown. What should have been a deep grey brick was covered in soot from nearby smokestacks. It was an eyesore compared to the Victorian houses around it.

Milo and I went around to the back, leaving Orion to go to the front door. Orion, with his small frame and little boy lost face, was by far the least threatening and therefore made contact first. He was what our leaders called the identifier.

Milo and I spotted the bicycle powered street vendor trailer that always waited for us in the back alley of a defect's house. This one was labeled with a sign: *Fortune Teller–hear your future for 15 pounds.* I sighed, thinking I'd pay way more than 15 pounds for one moment of my past. Not that I had 15 pounds. Our work was unpaid because we were working off what we owed our leaders for the new, special limbs we never asked for. The leaders told us that once we'd paid our debt, we'd be let go. How much we owed them, they wouldn't say. I asked Milo where people went once they left, and he told me no one had left since he'd been there.

"Did I choose this? Did you?" I asked.

Milo grunted. "Would they have taken away our memory if we'd chosen this?"

Since there was no iron gate, I twisted the doorknob and with a simple nudge of my arm, broke through the lock. That was the reason they gave us for needing new, improved limbs: rounding up these people required strength, but the defects didn't put up much of a fight. They were no match for our new limbs.

Milo and I crept up the backstairs, through the kitchen and down the hall. Our latest capture was opening the front door, and there was Orion.

"Are you Benjamin?" Orion asked, "Benjamin Ros—"

Before Orion could say the full name, Benjamin attempted to slam the door in his face. Orion was ready and blocked it with his arm.

Benjamin turned and ran down the hall, towards us. He slammed right into Milo. Orion grabbed Benjamin from behind. It took both Milo and Orion to hold him down. Benjamin kicked and twisted while I confirmed the number on his arm with the scanner on my sleeve.

The scanner flashed a green light. I pumped my fist and injected a dart into his arm.

Our captive continued to struggle for thirty more seconds. Thrashing about in Orion and Milo's arms, just before passing out, he shouted, "How can you do this? How can you do this to your fellow man? Cleaning us out like we're rats."

I looked closely at him, not because of what he said – they all said something like that and we were told to ignore it – no, I looked up because something about him smelled familiar. Before I could place it, he went limp.

I placed a spare pair of goggles over the captive's eyes. Milo and Orion both thought this detail was silly. The defect was out, eyes closed, but Creeping Green could still seep through.

Milo threw the defect over his shoulder and walked down the hall. Orion locked the front door and followed. My next job was to do a thorough search of the place, make sure that the captive had been home alone, that no one had been hiding. I worked quickly, starting with his living room, which was depressing. He obviously lived alone. There was one of everything: one coaster on the coffee table, one cast iron chair, and on the brown leather couch, one spot that sank in. A potbelly stove stood alone in the corner.

In the only bedroom, there was a locked wooden box under his bed. The lock was no match for the strength of my new fingers.

The items in the locked box were also underwhelming and depressing. A book with תּוֹרָה, meaning Torah, written on the front and a little black hat, way too small for our captive's head. A yarmulke. How the hell did I know that? And how did I know that the unfamiliar lettering meant Torah? Another book, in slightly better condition, had no name and was made of black leather. On the inside, pages were handwritten and dated. The last entry, dated a week before, read:

> If the rumors are true, it's happening again. People can't stop killing one another. Just like Stalin. Just like Mao. Just like Hitler. Zaideh said it would happen again if we weren't careful, if we stopped remembering the past. I'm glad he's not here to see another revolution killing off its culture, eating its intelligentsia.

"Riley? You find something?" Orion called from down the hall.

"No. Nothing."

I shoved the box back under the bed and did a quick search of the bedroom closet before making my way down the hall to the kitchen. A small room jutted out from the other side of the kitchen. While making my way there, I smelled it again, the familiar scent, the same one that was on our captive's breath.

I sniffed the thick bread on the counter. Wasn't it. Next to the bread was a glass container in a metal stand. It looked like one of the beakers used in the lab back at base. Inside was something that looked like dirt. It had the same scent as the latest defect's breath.

Next to the beaker was a small brown bag and inside it were beans with the same smell. I lifted the bag and dumped a few in my mouth, but they were too tough to chew. The smell was equally strong, with a hint of chocolate and hazelnut, like the fancy dessert we got at dinner on the nights we brought in a defect. The smell filled my mouth and made me thirsty. That feeling, that thirst was familiar. I couldn't let it go. Besides the Amy Winehouse music, it was the most familiar thing about this world. I shoved the paper bag into the pocket of my leather jacket even though we were on strict orders to only take defects, none of their belongings.

***

That night on base, I lingered in the dining hall after dinner, eating my dessert slowly. My comrades went to bed early because we had more combat training for our new limbs the next day.

Through the kitchen door, Cook glanced my way. He fancied me. Personally, I hated using the word fancy that way, it felt off somehow, but our leaders did, so I used it as a replacement for like to fit in. Besides it was true. Cook fancied me. Even with my memory wiped clean, I was still a woman and a woman always knows when she is fancied, ridiculous as the word or concept behind it sounds.

I did *not* fancy him, but had to know what was up with the strange beans from earlier that day. I walked into the kitchen where Cook was prepping tomorrow's breakfast, as close to the counter as his bulging stomach would allow. His head was almost as round and big as his belly and his nose folded out into the shape of a gas lamp.

I wondered what his real name was. None of the staff used real names on base. Cook was cook; maid was maid and so on. He didn't have our mechanical legs or arms and once I'd asked him if he was being rewarded or punished with this job. He'd said neither, that it was just a job. He wasn't one of us nor was he one of our leaders. He was Cook, which made me comfortable approaching him with my loot.

Without a word, I took out the small brown bag and slid it across the counter. Cook gave me a curious smile before looking inside. He took a long sniff. His smile grew wider.

"Where did you get this?"

I answered his question with a question, figuring it was better for both of us if he didn't know, "What is it?"

He took another sniff. "It smells stronger than Colombian. Definitely a dark roast."

"A roast?"

Cook laughed. He was the kind of man whose whole body shook when he laughed. "Not that kind of roast. Coffee."

He waited for the word to register, but it didn't. I wondered what he knew about me. Probably as little as I did, just that I wouldn't remember anything.

"People used to drink it like we drink our morning tea here, and it gives you a boast. It used to be very popular until it was outlawed. Queen Anne forbids anyone from selling it because it supposedly makes people too aggressive. You could get in a lot of trouble with this, doll."

I eyed the coffee while Cook eyed me. We both desired something in the room, and there was no use denying it. I wasn't getting something for nothing. Things around the base didn't work that way.

"I can make some for us and then, perhaps, afterwards, we can share something else," he said and locked the kitchen door.

I nodded. I'd been on that base long enough to know what he meant. Milo had been carrying on with one of my female comrades. She was in the bunker next to mine. Even though I didn't fancy Cook, it was worth it to experience this familiar smell, this coffee.

Cook filled a teakettle with water and put it on the gas stove. He poured the beans into a white container. He turned the handle of the white container forcefully and a hint of muscle appeared through the fat in his arm. He poured the ground beans into a beaker just like the one I'd seen in our captive's kitchen earlier that day.

The teakettle boiled and whistled. Something about that whistle made my knees lock and my eyes dart around the room.

"Does it always do that?" I yelled over the noise.

Cook nodded. He poured the smoking water from the teakettle into the beaker. Where had I heard that noise before? The whistling? It couldn't have been from here in the kitchen, which was separate from the rest of the base by thick concrete walls. Besides, my bunker was several feet down the hall.

Cook covered the beaker. "Now, we wait."

"How long?" I was anxious, my heart rate up thanks to that teakettle whistle.

"Seven minutes."

I watched the wheels winding within the clock above the stove. Cook watched me.

***

Exactly seven minutes later, Cook grabbed two of the cups used for morning tea and motioned toward a long metal table in the center of the kitchen. He brought over the beaker of coffee and poured us each a cup.

Soon as he poured mine, I went right for it, but he stopped me with his hand. "Slowly. It's hot. Sip it first."

He let his hand linger on mine until I pulled away.

After another minute, he showed me, putting his big mouth on that little cup and slowly taking in the coffee. But he didn't sip. He slurped. Loudly.

I brought the cup to my mouth. The heat from the coffee warmed my lips, nose, and cheeks. I closed my eyes and took in a sip. The taste was a jolt, even bolder than the smell.

I took another, slower sip and held it longer in my mouth. A hint of chocolate, something fruity, and a room…

***

A crowded room filled with small tables and a counter with people working behind it. There was that scent, coffee, everywhere. Across from me, a beautiful girl with long, curly, dark brown hair and eyes, exotically big and wide and violet, unlike any eyes I'd ever seen. Eyes so big and intense it was hard to see anything else. She was sitting across from me, smiling.

She said, "I do want to be with you, very much so, but that's not all I want. I want a family. And you'd need to want that, too, for this to work."

I opened my mouth to speak, but a woman's voice, calm yet urgent interrupted, "Color red, color red."

It was a recorded voice, repeating over and over. "Color red, color red." It interrupted the music that had been playing, music with horns and Amy Winehouse singing "*Cause what's inside her, it never dies*". And everyone, including the girl with the wild eyes, ran out of the room, out into the street. We were all outside surrounded by concrete and palm trees and a blistering light. The recorded voice repeated again, “Color red, color red.” The girl grabbed my hand. Then a whistle, like the teakettle, and a loud crash.

***

I opened my eyes. Having finished his coffee, Cook rubbed his groin with one hand, his eyes on my chest. I glanced down. There wasn’t much to look at; he had more of a chest than me.

That didn’t stop Cook. He pulled me up and took off my clothes, then his. He worked fast, the only good part about it. He laid me back on the table and rubbed against me for a minute. I closed my eyes again. At least Cook smelled of coffee and the chocolate, hazelnut dessert he’d made that evening for us.

I kept my mind on the girl sitting across the table, those eyes. The whole time he pushed against me, sending a sharp pain up my spine, I pictured the girl’s piercing eyes. Who was she? How did I know her?

***

Cook got dressed, washed his hands and went back to prepping breakfast. He turned to watch as I got dressed, but said nothing. I took the rest of the coffee, the whole glass container to my room and downed it slowly with my eyes closed. My heart raced as I tried to hold on to the girl, those eyes, the music, then the whistle, the woman’s voice, “Color red, color red.”

Another image came. The girl’s hair blowing in the wind, her arms around my waist as we rode a bicycle, except the bicycle had an engine and went faster, much faster. The girl leaned close. Her lips against my ear, she said, “Don’t stop.”

***

For the next six months, each time we went to pick up another defect in New Southampton, I kept an eye out for something that resembled the engine-powered bicycle in my vision. I asked Milo and Orion if they'd ever heard of such a thing. Neither had. I also listened for the recording, the woman's voice, for the whistling, for anything that resembled those images and noises in my head. Had I been hurt in some kind of attack? Was that how I ended up recruited for this army?

The questions and visions ate at me, the sound of the alarm and the woman repeating, "Color red, color red." The hissing and clanging of the pipes on base kept me up as well. I began to hate the stares Cook gave me, mirrored soon by my male and female comrades. He'd probably bragged to them. I kept my distance from him, knowing he could turn me in for the coffee at any time.

I walked the halls at night, tracing the hissing in the pipes to one room at the end of the hall. Its door was always locked. I'd listen at the door for a while every night. All I heard was a hum, steady and low. It was the room where our leaders convened before breakfast and after dinner. I was convinced that the answer to whatever they put in our heads and however they took away our memory was in that room.

***

One evening that suspicion was confirmed when Milo came back late. He had been sent out with two newer comrades to pick up a defect. His two comrades had returned with a defect, but without Milo. When he showed up, hours later, Milo reeked of cigars and fried foods, of a place like the Red Lion Pub.

Heinrich, Third-in-Command, sounded the bell for all of us to gather round.

"Behold your comrade," Heinrich grabbed Milo by his neck and pulled him up off the ground. Milo didn't react, didn't even seem to be in pain.

Heinrich glared right into Milo's eyes. His stare said it all. Heinrich was looking at a soon to be dead man.

Milo grinned and spat in Heinrich's face. Heinrich slammed Milo down to the ground.

He wiped Milo's spit off his sleeve before marching down the hall to the locked room. He waved his hand in front of a small black box on the wall. The door opened, revealing a machine as wide and tall as one side of the room. The machine had a low, steady hum.

Not able to stand still, I forced my way in front of my comrades, wanting to stop Heinrich, but not sure how. One foolish move and I'd end up on the ground next to Milo. That wouldn't do anyone any good.

Heinrich grabbed the lever with Milo's name on it and yanked it down. Our eyes turned back to Milo. His body shook. White foam dripped from his mouth.

Two seconds later he was completely still on the ground, eyes wide. He was gone.

My comrades and I, about two dozen of us in all, watched as the janitor carried Milo down to the other end of the hall to an elevator that went above ground. I wondered where they would dispose of the body, what they would try to make it look like. It was the first murder I'd seen since I'd been there. It wasn't going to be the last unless I did something.

***

First, I had to be more cautious. Before Milo's death, along with pacing the halls, I'd asked our leaders questions that no one else dared. So I stopped pacing and asking questions and just went about my business.

Perhaps the leaders noticed my change in attitude, or so I thought, because a week later they put me in charge of the next pick up. I was under strict orders to enter the address alone. Orion was to wait out back for me to come out with the defect. No exceptions.

The whole monorail ride, I sulked, mad at myself for thinking the leaders had some newfound faith in me. On the way out, they'd given me the name of the new defect. Violet. They weren't rewarding me or noticing my new, upbeat attitude. The only reason they'd put me in charge was because the defect was a woman.

Orion read the card with the name and address in my hand. "No last name this time. That's a first," he said.

Orion kept staring at the card. I closed my hand around it. The name on the card made me think of the girl from my visions, those wild eyes. The name made me nervous.

"Do you ever wonder what happens to them?" I asked.

Orion shook his head. “You saw what they did to Milo. It’s best just to do what we’re told and not think about anything.”

I realized then that it was risky even asking Orion questions. He could warn Heinrich that I was too curious. I’d end up like Milo.

As usual, we got off at a northern New Southampton station and walked right past the nicer part of the neighborhood. Creeping Green hung low that night. I tightened my goggles. Every time we came above ground, it seemed like the smog grew greener and thicker. A couple of elderly people without goggles walked right into us, confirming our suspicion that Creeping Green seeps into the eyeballs and causes blindness.

We got to 1069 Hanover where a red flag hung out a second story window. Instead of the usual rundown flat, this was a Victorian house with gas lamps in the windows, all burning brightly.

Orion smirked.

“What?” I asked.

“Milo told me about places like this,” he said.

I wondered how Milo knew more than we did. He’d probably gone on previous drinking excursions. Milo never said it, but it was obvious that he didn’t like following rules.

Orion slumped toward the alley with a warning, “Don’t do anything Milo would do.” He winked, but disappointment was dripping from his voice. He liked the action that came with taking a new defect, especially female – although he never said anything like that to me. He’d say it to Milo when he thought I wasn’t listening, but now Milo was gone.

Inside, the house was dark with heavy shadows from the gas lamps. A giant wheel clock hung over the fireplace. Curtains draped the entrance to every room and hallway. A tall, dark skinned woman in a skin-tight, black velvet suit greeted me just inside the door.

“Is Violet here?” I asked after removing my goggles.

The woman was not surprised to see me. “I don’t need any trouble here. So whatever business you have with her, take care of it quietly and exit out the back.”

I nodded.

She led me through a curtain and down a hall, past more curtains where I heard noises like I’d heard from Milo and that female recruit.

The woman stopped in front of a royal blue curtain and motioned for me to go inside. She disappeared quickly, back to the front of the house.

On the other side of the curtain, a woman had her back to me. She had on a corset, short skirt, garter and black tights. Her shoulders were exposed, her skin naturally tan. Her dark brown hair danced off her shoulders, down her back.

She turned around and those eyes flickered at me. They were even more striking there by candlelight – the only light in the tiny room – than they had been in my visions. Dots began to connect in my mind. Violet eyes, hence the name.

Had I been sent there on purpose? As a kind of a test? Put in charge of this mission, not because she was a woman, but because she was *the* woman? I opened my mouth, but couldn't speak. If only I could remember more.

Those wide eyes filled with tears, but she fought them off. She sat on the bed with a sigh. "I really hoped you were dead."

"Dead?" The nerve. This girl – the girl in my vision – a few years older, a woman now, she hoped I was dead. Her eyes, still on the verge of tears, gave her away though.

"You'd be better off. And so would I." She didn't mean it. She looked down because she knew her eyes had betrayed her.

"I don't understand," I said.

"You don't *remember*." She put a blouse on over her corset and suddenly I did remember something – a mole above her hip, another below her breast.

"I remember some things."

"Like what?"

I took a step back and made a fist. I had to bring her back or they'd pull the lever and kill me. Then they'd send someone else to get her.

"I've seen you before. We were in some type of restaurant, having coffee and an alarm went off. Everyone ran and there were explosions."

Violet leaned back on the bed, propping herself up with her hands. She crossed her legs. I wondered how many she'd laid down with in that bed. My fist grew tighter.

Her body softened and she raised her eyes to meet mine. "We met in Tel Aviv. Your parents were missionaries. They didn't count on you falling in love."

"With you," I said.

Violet exploded with a laugh that filled the room. "And Tel Aviv, that café, the strong coffee, the music the owner always played, the weather, the bright sun. You didn't want to leave Tel Aviv, but we had to. You couldn't handle it."

"Handle what?"

Violet stood up and walked toward me. She was close. So close, I could smell vanilla in her hair, sandalwood on her skin.

"The alarms. The bombings. The uncertainty of an ongoing feud that goes back a lot further than this current war. You developed what doctors there call *charada*—"

"Severe anxiety." If I could remember what certain words meant, then maybe I could remember everything.

Her eyes grew wide, hopeful. "Yes, a kind of post traumatic stress. Yours was extreme. When you got anxious, you became this monster, someone I didn't recognize. So we came here, which was peaceful at the time. We opened a café in New Southampton, which I ran by myself after you got sick."

"Sick?"

"Yes, all the anxiety medicines you were on made your kidneys fail. That's how Heinrich and his group of neo-Nazis recruited you. They took you from the hospital in the middle of the night. They take all the recruits from the hospital and replace whatever organs are betraying them with organs from my people," Violet said.

A wave of nausea took over me. I was alive and healthy thanks to the organs, thanks to the death of a defect. No wonder Violet wanted me dead.

"Why?"

"They're building an army to rid the world of my people while everyone else is distracted by the war. I've worked here ever since our café was closed due to the Queen's new ordinance. This place has kept me safe, off the radar," she said.

I stepped away from Violet, my back touching the curtain door to the room, my foot almost in the hall. Remember why you're here, Riley, I reminded myself. Sweat formed in between my clinched fingers.

Violet stepped toward me. "This isn't what it looks like. I'm not having sex with just anyone."

"Just whoever shows up and pays?" I asked.

Her hand ripped across my face.

She stepped back from me and said, "The group you're with won't stop until they kill all of us. This is my way of fighting back, making sure my people aren't all extinct." Her hand fell to her belly. Even though I still didn't remember much, I knew what *that* gesture meant.

My arm tightened. My breath grew tight. I saw nothing but Violet, Violet with random men. "If you loved me, you wouldn't be here, doing this, no matter what the reason."

"This has nothing to do with you," she said.

Before I lost my nerve, I grabbed her, and scanned the numbers on her arm. She didn't fight, didn't even struggle. Her eyes were wide. Her faced stunned. She couldn't believe that I was taking her in. When the green light flashed on my sleeve, I pumped my fist and shot a needle right into her arm.

***

"She's pregnant," the physician informed Heinrich outside the infirmary on base. Listening from the table at the edge of the dining hall, it only confirmed what I already suspected. Violet was with child due to some crazed, noble agenda, but why couldn't the leaders do to her what they did with the other people we brought in: kill her and use her parts. All the defects we'd been sent to grab had certain things in common. They'd all been in their twenties or thirties, all healthy, single, alone, and none of the women before Violct had been pregnant, so maybe killing a pregnant woman would distort something in their fucked up moral code.

The question remained what would they do with her. There was no taking her back to where she worked. She knew about them, us. And Violet was not the type of girl who'd keep her mouth shut.

I forced myself to eat. Heinrich had men walk around and watch us eat. They'd ask us questions if they noticed we didn't have much of an appetite. They were constantly observing us to see if our work with the defects was getting to us.

I pretended to savor every bite of the chocolate, hazelnut dessert, but inside something took over my body. Thinking about what they'd do to Violet, my breath quickened, my eyes couldn't focus.

An alarm went off on a comrade's watch at a dinner table nearby and I jumped up out of my seat. I walked toward Heinrich and the physician. Walking to my death was one thing, but one wrong move also meant the end of Violet and the baby.

"Something wrong with the captive I brought in?" I managed to keep my voice even and calm. Heinrich nodded for the physician to return to the infirmary and motioned for me to follow.

He headed toward the room at the end of the hall. This was it. He was going to pull my lever. I wasn't going to be able to save Violet. I couldn't even save myself. My body clenched up. I waited for the bell, the signal for the recruits to come watch my death, but it never rang. Instead, Heinrich took me inside the room at the end of the hall and the door closed behind us.

There was the machine with the low, steady hum. There were the other leaders, Heinrich's bosses, the second and first in command sitting at a square table. Behind them was another room, smaller. While Heinrich entered it, I checked out the seven-foot machine with all the levers. In the lower right hand corner was a lever with my name on it.

"Impressive, isn't it?" Second-in-Command said. "One little lever shuts down the chip we put in your brain which is connected to your central nervous system, and then everything shuts down."

This was my chance to get information, anything to help my comrades, to help myself. I studied the machine and said, "It is impressive. Must take a lot of power. What happens if the electricity goes out or the machine breaks? You lose your whole army?"

Second-in-Command glanced at First-in-Command who nodded. Second-in-Command continued, "No, of course not. The machine has a built in program to shut itself down if something should happen. The chip in your head will become inactive at that time."

Somehow I had built their trust or they were testing me with this information. They're smugness about having all bases covered irritated me. A null and void chip would still be in our heads. Would our memories still be gone?

Before I could ask anything else, Heinrich came back into the room carrying a gun with a small wheel in its center. "We haven't trained you on this yet," he said, showing it to me. "But it's pretty simple."

With his thumb, he showed me how I cocked it by spinning the wheel back and when I pulled the trigger, the wheel would spin forward, releasing the bullet. I wiped my sweaty palms on my pants. My only thought, echoing like a mantra: Give me the gun, give me the gun.

"Yes, pretty simple," I said.

Heinrich loaded one bullet in the gun.

"Can you add a couple more? One might not do the trick," I said as neutrally as possible.

The leaders glanced at each other and snickered.

"So you know what we need you to do?" First-in-Command asked.

"Yes. She's unusable and since I brought her in, it's my responsibility," I said, and repeated in my head, give me the gun.

"We could wait until she delivers," Second-in-Command suggested to the others.

"What would we do with one of their babies on our hands?" First-in-Command asked, but it wasn't really a question. "We'd have to wait years before we could use it."

Heinrich finished loading the bullets and gave me the gun.

First-in-Command turned to me, "Riley, we want to make you captain, in charge of your comrades. And your first duty as captain is to protect them. You are protecting them by killing this whor—"

First-in-Command didn't finish his sentence because I shot him right in the mouth. Second-in-Command lunged for me but I kicked him across the room using the leg he'd given me. His back slammed into the concrete wall and snapped. The echo of the snap bounced around the room.

Something in me had snapped. I was stronger than I thought possible, stronger than I'd ever been while practicing combat moves on base or out capturing defects.

Heinrich grabbed my throat. I grasped at his arms, I gasped for air.

The room began to spin. I closed my eyes. I thought about what his physician would do to Violet. Then my mind flashed to a doctor telling me of the dangers of charada if I didn't take medication to control it. A severe anxiety that creates an uncontrollable rage, the doctor had said. I'd told him that I didn't want to take his prescription, his medicine. Charada was part of me.

Heinrich gripped my throat tighter. That's when I let it in; let the rage take over, up my legs and through my arms and down my back.

I thrust Heinrich over my shoulders and slammed him onto the concrete floor. He wouldn't give up. From the floor, he reached up for my lever. But I wound the gun and shot him in the head.

Two seconds later my comrades pounded on the door. They'd heard the gunshots. I thought about the physician. He'd get nervous and do something to Violet.

If I pressed the button to open the door to the room, Heinrich's henchmen would have access to the machine. The same henchmen who watched us eat every meal.

I looked at the machine and thought about how Heinrich and his men had taken away all my memories of Violet, of my life. I grabbed the machine from the side and thought about the first thing Violet said to me earlier that day. How she had hoped I was dead. If Second-in-Command was lying to me, I would be.

With my new limbs and all the rage from not having my memories, I pulled the machine from the wall. Using all my strength I pushed it over, on top of Heinrich. The machine was so heavy the room shook when it hit.

The low, steady hum was gone. The room was silent. The lights flickered. A stream of Heinrich's blood ran along the side of the machine.

I felt nothing. And then, ten seconds later, I felt everything. I remembered.

I remembered how Violet had lost both her parents in a war with Hezbollah, how her father had named her after those eyes even though her mother had warned him that the eye color of a newborn often changes. I remembered a dance club and a live band, which had a horn section, a saxophone solo and the first time she danced close to me.

I remembered our first kiss, after a motorcycle ride where she'd wanted me to keep going, keep driving. I'd wanted to stop on a hill along the way, but because I'd kept going, when I finally dropped Violet off at her house, she'd rewarded my good behavior with our first kiss.

Violet.

I opened the door. My comrades were fighting Heinrich's henchmen in the hall and winning. Their mechanical arms gave them an advantage against the men who had showed us how to use them. Running down the hall, I dodged the fighting. I had to get to Violet, Violet and her baby.

When I got to the infirmary, Heinrich's physician was about to stick a needle in Violet's arm. Violet was awake and trying to push him away, but she was tied to the operating table.

I shot him in the chest. Violet jerked her head around, not surprised at all to see me.

I untied her from the table. She sat up slowly, looking down the hall at my comrades attempting to beat some answers out of Heinrich's men.

"You start all this?" she asked. She was calm, unafraid of the chaos and violence, because she grew up around it.

"The guys in charge wanted me to kill you," I said.

Violet moved to the edge of the bed. Her hand fell to her belly. Her face relaxed as she realized the baby was all right.

Her eyes warmed even that room, a room in which so many people had died. Her mouth's normal position was that of a frown, but that only made her smile all the more meaningful. I looked over her body, its winding, never-ending curves. I looked for something wrong, something defective that would make others hate her. All I saw was beautiful.

"You remember," she said.

"How do you know?"

"Because you're looking at me the way you used to, the way that made me excited and nervous at the same time." This time Violet didn't fight the tears.

She attempted to stand up, but she was still dizzy from the drug I'd injected her with, and she fell back against the table. I went to her. Wrapping my arms around her, her soft skin, her touch, her scent – sandalwood and vanilla, everything was familiar. She ran her hands along my arms, squeezed them, feeling the metal just beneath my flesh. She rested her hands on my face. "It doesn't matter what they've done to you, you're still mine."

I picked her up and carried her out of the room. We walked by my comrades, including Orion, who were now organizing Heinrich's men, putting them in chains. I glanced into to the kitchen. Cook was packing up his supplies as fast as his round body could move.

I carried Violet down the dark hall to the elevator. We tightened our goggles as the monorail pulled into the station. We raced through the streets, past the Amy Winehouse statue. Word would get out that the base was destroyed and whoever worked with Heinrich's group would want answers. We had to move fast. I glanced back at the Winehouse statue, realizing that I might not see New Southampton again.

Violet regained her strength and led the way, first down a side street, then through an alley to another alley and finally to a padlocked garage. She searched under a stack of bricks for the spare key.

"No need." I ripped off the lock with my fingers.

The half-smile gave her away. She didn't want to be impressed, but she was.

Inside the dark garage was a bicycle with a motor, exactly like the one I'd seen in my visions.

"Remember how to drive it?" Violet asked.

I draped a leg over it. I turned the key, pulled up the kickstand and nodded with confidence.

Violet shook her head and tossed me a helmet. I stared at it, unable to remember a time when I wore one.

"Okay, maybe I don't remember everything," I said.

Violet put on hers. "You never liked wearing them, but you will now."

She grabbed a leather bag out of the metal chest in the corner before hopping on behind me. I glanced back at the bag while adjusting my helmet.

"Money from selling the café. Enough to live on for a while," she said.

Thirty seconds later we were taking side streets, the same side streets I'd walked down with Orion and Milo. We followed them out of New Southampton, away from the Creeping Green.

Violet's arms were wrapped around my waist, lips right next to my ear. All I heard, as the wind ripped through our hair was her voice, "Don't stop."

The two words were more urgent than when she'd first said them, years ago, because things were different now. Violet was pregnant. I had the limbs Heinrich and his men gave me. And I had something else, an unstoppable rage that it was time to embrace and use. If I owned it, owned charada, I could use it to protect Violet, her baby, her people, and people everywhere who were being persecuted.

SIMON SIMPLE

by
Nancy Hansen

Simon crouched in the shadows as two of the City Guard rode by. They should not see him; no one usually could unless he wanted them to, but he had learned never to tempt fate. He was not of course entirely invisible, just outwardly patterned like the cold stone of the building behind him, and so, easily overlooked. The masked and uniformed men with lanterns and truncheons pedaled their high wheel velocipedes within mere feet of his position. He held his breath; barely daring to exhale as they passed, then turned his head ever so slowly, watching them move on before detaching himself from a rather convenient pool of darkness just out of the range of the nearest gaslight along the cobbled street. With a swirl of his cloak, he disappeared into the night again.

The cloak was rather an ostentatious thing, but it was the chosen outerwear of the gentry, and the Thieves Guild had adopted it as an official nose-thumbing of their betters. It was handy in a downpour and on blustery, frosty nights, when even the Creeping Green vapors—popularly nicknamed CG and pronounced 'CeeGee' on the street— parted just enough that one might see a momentary patch of sky. Full moonlight made the thick miasma around him glow in emerald splendor, pretty enough if you could get past the fact that it was noxious and would ruin your lungs and brain without a proper filtering mask. No one in his right mind went outdoors for more than a moment without donning one, except perhaps Cyrus

Mayweather, and that explained quite a bit about the madman of the shuttered byways. Simon settled his hat, tightened the face straps, readjusted his goggles, and moved on.

His destination was far closer to the marketplace than he preferred to be. Too many Mayweather sympathizers skulking around there at night, and they were always trouble. Cyrus and his far too inbred clan were something Simon had been forced to leave behind or risk becoming just as deranged as they were. A foundling left on the scrap heaps, he was named 'Simon Kaylocke' for the Mayweather family he was given to. The Kaylockes raised and indoctrinated him into Mayweather illicit activities, training him in the art of rebellious anarchy of the most brutal type; but he'd never become one of them.

The Mayweathers had abandoned him when the Regulators showed up too soon during his last mission, leaving young Simon bleeding and shivering in the winter cold beneath a pile of blast rubble and dead bodies. He survived and moved into the poorest part of the city, changing his name and eking out a living begging and stealing. Simon knew he was better off being thought dead, as the Mayweathers would never let someone who understood so many of their secrets simply walk away. He was forced to use the same chameleonic talents that made him a clan favorite to avoid them while making a new life for himself.

He didn't enjoy robbery and strong arm coercion, but a man had to eat, which is why he was out this night, calling on patrons with debts to a local dice parlor. There had been a recent raid by the Regulators, and in the confusion, a few regulars had skipped out without paying up. The pit boss reported them, and as soon as he opened shop elsewhere, the owner contracted Simon Simple as a free agent enforcer. It wasn't pleasant work, but steady, and there was a landlady to pay, who as long as the rent was on time, never asked questions or whispered into the wrong ears.

His first mark was a solicitor of some means. The man should be well asleep by now so it was time to wake the high-rolling fool and make sure he was given a good fright. Simon would not harm him, just shake him up and remind him that debts were to be paid in full and on time. This was why he had been chosen for the job. The curly haired young man who called himself, "Simon, simply Simon," was one of the most successful underworld enforcers. He was efficient in getting people to pay up, yet he never left a trail of dead or broken bodies behind him.

Well hidden in the shadows surrounding a service entrance, Simon pulled his lock picks and expertly popped the mechanism on the outer door without clanging the attached bell. He let himself into the airlock vestibule. Waiting for the pressure to equalize so that none of the CG was allowed to seep in, he counted to twenty, and then fiddled with the inner lock. Once inside, his mask went into the belt bag and the goggles got pushed up on his hat. Grinning rakishly, he withdrew a calling card from a small leather case in his pocket, and left it in the hall tray. That was a little something he had come up with on his own. On a black background was a skull pierced by a stiletto, surrounded by small blue flowers. Lifting the skull, inside it read: *Forget me not, or fate shall seek to call anon.* The illicit cards were expensive, but chillingly effective in reminding deadbeats that if Simon Simple had gotten inside once, he could do it again; and he'd be armed.

This man reportedly lived alone. Other than avoiding a rather noisy small dog, who was satisfied enough with a rind of greasy pastry to allow itself to be shooed in the pantry, Simon was able to bound up the winding stairs to the upper level unnoticed. On the way he pinched a set of small but exquisite silver candlesticks that would trade well, and discarded all but one candle stub.

Thankfully the bedroom door was only shut and not bolted. Simon let himself in quietly and cat-footed it to the curtained bedside, where he warily watched the snoring sleeper. The hearth was cold, the fire long since gone out and coals banked, for the convoluted chimneys that kept out the noxious green gas made for a bad draft and smoke indoors at night.

He lit the candle stub from an ember and set it on a dresser, where it would give some back lighting but not illuminate his face. A pitcher of water and a tumbler sat on the nightstand. He grabbed the handle of the pitcher. It seemed nice and cold. Good for a wakeup call then…

The sudden splash had the man sputtering and cursing as he abruptly sat up in bed. His frightened eyes widened as they caught sight of a shadowy figure almost blending with the bed drapes. Whoever it was who had so rudely awakened him leaned backward against the bedpost, tall booted legs crossed as he very nonchalantly trimmed his fingernails with a stiletto.

"Who are you? What do you want of me?" the man said with a bluster that barely concealed his quaking fright. He pulled the sodden quilt up to his chin.

"I've come to remind you to pay your debts," Simon said in a low and threatening tone that was all but unrecognizable. "On the morrow you will go down to Byerly Street and ask for the clerk of Morgan Mather. Your account is in his book. You will pay him in full, with interest. If you don't," Simon spun the blade around his fingers, a trick he'd learned from one of his Mayweather compatriots, "I'll come back and collect it for Master Mather myself. I won't bother waking you next time."

A swish of the cloak and slice of stiletto, and the candle went out. By the time the frightened man became brave enough to climb out of bed, Simon was downstairs, yanking on his mask and goggles before letting himself back out into the night. When the man tiptoed down after his would-be assailant with a heavy cane in hand, Simon was long gone.

Simon slipped into the night, satisfied with his performance. They usually paid up after one visit, so he'd seldom had to resort to a second appearance, and never to actual violence, which would bring the Regulators sniffing around. He'd get paid once Mather did, but the candlesticks would see him through. Such metal was a rare find outside the palace. He stashed them in a safe spot he knew of and moved on.

Heading down Lime Way, he picked an alley with a fence that was easy to scale. He was just on the other side of it looking for a particular balcony when a familiar figure in form fitting brown leather vaulted down from the window ledge above, landing lightly in a crouch in front of him. The voice was muffled beneath the mask, but it said gruffly, "Fancy meeting you here, Love!"

"Mattie," he said with consternation, which the mask made sound wheezy. "What are you doing here?" It was a merchant neighborhood, but none of them were particularly wealthy. Not healthy pickings for such as she.

Mattie Fox leaned in close, whispering. "Passing on a friendly warning. Eli Kirkland is around, and he's been asking nosy questions about our kind."

Well, that was going to put a damper on the evening! Muscle-bound Eli was a bounty hunter known for his ruthlessness. His presence suggested that someone had issued a *"dead is as good as alive"* edict for those of special talents. Simon had no doubts he was also a target.

"So why is Eli hunting us—and for whom?" he asked her quickly. There was a measured tread on the cobbles of the narrow roadway, but it was likely just a flatfoot 'Reggie', or another prowler. He lost it in the rumble of the monorail as it passed by, but out of habit began moving back toward the shadows.

She smiled and leaned in. "There's a big shakeup coming. The word is, the lot of us is to be rounded up and executed by orders of Her Most Royal Pain-In-The-Bum. Something about quelling a rebellion."

"I'm no rebel. How do I figure into this?" he asked, knowing he wasn't getting the entire story. Mattie was as close to a friend as he had on the streets, but Simon didn't totally trust her.

She leaned in conspiratorially. "You're special too, Simon. 'Sides, Kirkland's known to sell out to the highest bidder. P'raps the Mayweathers want you gone before the Regulators find out your talents go beyond picking pockets and shaking down gamblers. You know too much and if tortured they figure you'll sing like a regular clockwork canary. The Regulators are easy enough to avoid, Ducks, but Eli is going to be tough to ditch. He's quite proficient at hunting people down. I would make myself scarce for a while, were I you." Mattie's advice was usually sound.

"I can disappear when I need to," Simon reminded her.

"As can I, and far easier than you. But he's well equipped, that's why I came to warn you. Something about 'heat signatures' and 'goggles'—that's all the information I could squeeze out of my turnips; but it's enough. If he can see us, then he can get us. I'd love to pinch a pair of those things for myself though," she said with a half-smirk.

Something didn't make sense. The Mayweathers would not have given Eli Kirkland a set of advanced goggles; even if they could afford them, they had no use for such things. Kirkland had a far larger agenda.

"Where was Eli last seen?" he asked pointedly, wondering if he should just pack up and leave now, though where to go was an issue.

"Over past Spitalfields Avenue, on Petticoat Terrace last eve. He was rounding up the flesh peddlers and questioning them about our kind."

She would say no more, and Simon didn't press. Mattie had her contacts, and he had his, and the unspoken rule was, you didn't reveal your source. Spitalfields was the edge of the red lantern district and Petticoat Terrace was in the heart of it. He'd heard rumors there was an insurgent base somewhere in there, but the Rebel Underground didn't interest him much. Did they have Mattie's attention though?

"You know a safe house, I take it?" he asked her.

She hesitated before saying, "I might. Comes with a price though–"

He wasn't to find out anything else that night. There came a sudden, vigorous and shuddering burst of a hand cannon from the street outside their alley. They ran in opposite directions.

Mattie hit a brick wall and simply melted into it. "Phasing" is what she called it, that first time he had seen her do it. She seemed limited to certain porous materials only, but as she said, it was handy in their profession. All her gear went with her. The "talented" learned quickly that an intimate association with your body sort of rubbed off on your things.

There was shouting ahead, too close to run from without being seen, so Simon flattened himself against an inset door, feeling the familiar tingle as his body blended in with the blocks. He waited to see who came by.

Two "Evols"— the street moniker for Transhumans, their lack of goggles and masks as well as their flawless appearance, superior musculature and height, and ageless appearance all giving them away—preceded a squad of well-armed Regulators along the hastily vacated street. Simon had heard of Evols being used as Wintersmith's hounds, but this was the first evidence he'd seen of it. It seemed like everyone was out hunting tonight. Someone must be fetching a good head price.

"There are unnatural beings around," one of the Evols declared in his androgynous, echoing voice, while his face betrayed no sense of emotion.

Isn't that the pot calling the kettle black? So they are specifically hunting down mutants.

The Evols were actively casting about, so Simon didn't linger. Fading back into the darkness, he flipped his goggles to night vision and headed on. He left the area in the opposite direction that Mattie had taken, which is why he didn't learn of her situation until later on.

***

Mattie Fox was just flowing out of the building into the night when someone grabbed her by the forearm. She yanked back, but her captor was strong. She could not draw the other body in with her, she was just hoping to smash whoever it was against the building and be done with it. The sting of a blade edge tapping her exposed wrist said she'd end up with one hand less should she not capitulate, so she allowed herself be pulled back into the open. She might well lose that hand later anyway, as her transgressions were well documented. Queen Anne and her cronies at court had gone back to the old corporal and capital punishments of yore. Well, better later than now!

"Hello, Matilda darling," blond and square jawed Eli Kirkland greeted her as he smirked beneath his mask, which was dominated by some sort of advanced optic goggle that hid the bright blue of his eyes. Sheathing his saber, he grabbed her roughly by both arms and slapped a band of the long forgotten material called "plastique" around her wrists, tying them firmly behind her back. He snugged it taut enough to cut off the circulation to her hands, and yanked her about by the other end. She could not pass through that foreign compound of another age as she might with brass or iron cuffs. Eli had come prepared to deal with her specifically.

"What's this all about?" she queried as he dragged her along, shoving her roughly toward a Regulator steam gaol wagon. They had it lead and antimony plated of course. Lead was one of those materials Mattie had trouble with, because it lingered inside to poison the body. Antimony only made it harder.

"I've no idea, other than you're officially under arrest for crimes against the Crown. My part is done once I get paid," he added amiably enough as he frisked her, taking her burglary tool belt and any personal effects, before turning her over to her gaolers. They pushed her up a ramp, and fastened the end of her lead into a hook in the roof of the vehicle before shutting the tailgate. She was left dangling painfully by her arms, her similarly shackled feet barely reaching the floor. It was impossible to shift positions and exerted just enough stretching to be painful and wearying, without doing permanent damage.

"Have a lovely ride," Eli called out cheerily as the noisy steam engine started. The gaol wagon jerked and hissed, hooted and puffed, before jouncing away, with her forlorn figure bobbing uncomfortably inside. In the green half light of dawn, a few early risers or furtive late goers turned to peer curiously at whomever was being hauled off to prison this time.

Mattie swore under her breath, cursing her luck. She had come to warn Simon, and had gotten herself nabbed instead. She hoped at least he'd escaped notice, for there were far too few of their kind left in the city, with the current crackdown.

They'll not keep me in their lockup too long!

***

Avoiding the retreating sounds of a gaol wagon siren, Simon left the area unmolested, moving swiftly through back allies and byways he knew from his Mayweather days. He was a bit rattled, but raids happened all the time, and he still had work to do before daylight.

The second deadbeat was a couple blocks over. He was halfway there when he heard the tramp of numerous feet in heavy boots—another Regulator patrol. They weren't usually about this late in such force! He turned, but there was a rolling patrol coming the opposite way with a monowheel officer in their midst. He was trapped between them!

Simon hesitated only long enough to melt into the narrow confines of the space between jostling buildings, where piles of stinking refuse afforded him at least some cover. It was a shallow alleyway at best, and backed by a rather smooth brick wall that was far too high to climb in such a hurry. He'd not brought along his grapple and line, so he did his best to blend in as the men stopped right in front of his position.

"D'ya see someone goin' in there?" one of the men, a patrol

sergeant from his large badge, said to the leader of the other group.

"Might be the one as got away when we copped the Gasser lass. Send a trooper in with a lantern, and have your arms at ready." He raised his regulation cap and ball pistol, while others drew their swords.

The "Gasser lass?" They might have caught Mattie! Simon had no time to puzzle it out. A young trooper in the standard red and black leather of the Regulators, with one of their cheapest all-in-one mask and goggles strapped over his face, stalked uneasily back toward where he now hid. The youth held a truncheon in one hand, a lantern in the other. He was nervous, his heavy breathing puffing the thin canvas cover of the mask in and out as the carbon can struggled to filter breath mixed with the sweat dribbling down his face.

Simon eased himself up against the wall and slipped out his stiletto. He didn't plan to hurt the lad, but if he was discovered he'd have no choice but to take him as a hostage to bargain for his own life. Thankfully this raw recruit looked neither well armed nor sure of himself. Wintersmith must be cutting funding to the street guard again. Hopefully they'd parley and not shoot through the youngster to get Simon himself.

The ill-fated Regulator was within a few yards of the patterned form of a man pressed against the bricks when Simon leaned back. Something went "CLICK" and suddenly the ground beneath seemed to give way. A section of pavement tilted in and he tumbled feet first into a hole. He had the presence of mind not to cry out as he slid down inside a long, curving tube of a tunnel. The hatchway over him snapped shut.

***

The first two floors of the building was formerly a courthouse until Her Royal Majesty, Queen Anne Eliza Wintersmith, came to power. She took it as her own, having the bulk of her iron palace built atop and around it. The self-proclaimed Queen was the law now. She was having nearby buildings razed, replacing them with curtain walls and a great barbican gate on the main avenue, all made of dark iron slag blocks with rubble sandwiched between. The lesser gates were manned by temporary towers. It all had an austere, Gothic look to it. Inside was her private residence, barracks, an armory, meeting hall, guest suites, and deep beneath, storage areas and secure bunkers for shelter in case of extreme civil unrest, along with a brand new area of confinement for choice prisoners.

Mattie had fainted after being suspended so long in that uncomfortable position, so she had only dim memories of being hauled out of the gaol wagon and into a hidden portal somewhere on the now sprawling palace grounds. Were they ever going to be done adding on to it?

She was mildly surprised not to be dragged off to Eastleigh tower, but then, they had probably figured she'd be difficult to contain and would have more public exposure there. Either way, no one would come for her, so unless she could somehow break free on her own, she was as good as dead.

Where Mattie was being kept now was once the Zeppelin raid shelter of the original Southampton Courthouse, now renovated into some form of dungeon. They pushed her stumbling figure through first one airlock and then another farther along. Once inside, her mask and goggles were ripped off and tossed aside and she was patted down again. She got glimpses of other cells, occupied and empty, and brand new devices of torture being constructed as they hustled her along. Some poor bloke was lashed prone on a long contraption that looked suspiciously like a medieval rack. He screamed in agony as she was dragged by. A table of inquisitors were questioning him between turns of the device. She shivered in fear, and her grinning guards left her gawking a few moments before prodding her onward.

Her own cell was far in the rear. It reminded her of a closed diving bell. The men with her removed her ties while facility guards fiddled with some sort of locking device before she was unceremoniously shoved inside. The door shut with a reverberating clang and was fastened tight by a spinning wheel door lock. It was lowered by a great winch down into sort of a pit surrounded by a moat enclosure.

Inside it was far quieter. Mattie recognized the hissing and whumping noise of a steam pump starting up nearby. They must be filling the dead space with water—a futile incentive to keep her from trying to escape as she could pass through that without even phasing. She stood in the darkness rubbing her tortured arms and shoulders, waiting for the right moment.

Once she had the circulation back into her arms and the torment of torn muscles and overstretched tendons had subsided to a constant burning and nagging throb, she stumbled around, inspecting her cell carefully. The inside walls were slick and perpendicular, and while she could pass a hand through the first few inches, there was enough lead and antimony plating beyond that would make it unhealthy to do so. There was only one area that didn't have the multiple layers, but it was high up one wall, and all but impossible to climb even if she still had the cat's paw gloves and crampons that helped her find purchase on such surfaces. The would-be aperture appeared to be some sort of glass viewing port, and what was floating around beyond it was especially troubling. There was no mistaking that color, even in the darkness.

Creeping Green. They had surrounded her specialized cell with an entire enclosure of CG, knowing she wouldn't dare pass through lead and then into that expanse of deadly gas without a proper mask and goggles. It was diabolical but brilliant. Certainly Her Majesty had spared no expense to keep her confined. They had planned this for some time then.

The question was… why?

***

Regaining his feet, Simon could hear the light skittering of vermin, and the heavier shuffling sounds of things he would not want to accidentally meet in the inky darkness. He dipped into a vest pocket and pulled out his hand torch. With the flick of a lever, a whir, and a few rattles of the magnet inside the copper coil, he had just enough light to see a few feet around him. It also made him a target, but better that than falling into an unseen hole or tripping over something and braining himself on the narrow brickwork surrounding him.

He wasn't sure if it was pure chance that had opened the hidden hatchway near the brick wall, but Simon was grateful not to be stuck in a firefight with Regulators. With just a stiletto, he was woefully outclassed. What little he could make out of the heavily buttressed corridor he'd landed in was full of undisturbed dust and cobwebs, showing it had not been used in ages. It appeared to be an old access way for the city workers of yore, and likely now a forgotten part of that subterranean warren of mazes most of the thieves' quarter used as highway system. The arched ceiling was low, the brickwork old with mortar crumbling, and long roots poked through in a few places.

Even underground, his sense of direction was good, so Simon slipped gradually toward an outlet on the poorer side of town, ghosting past side tunnels that lead further into the bowels of the great maze. Now and then he flattened out to blend into the walls and doused his torch as voices or other stealthy footsteps drifted by where he encountered cross tunnels. Once past the busier areas, he was glad for the mask. Even without CG, the outlet he chose meandered down along a ditch filled with street runoff bobbing with rafts of sewage and offal. There was a very narrow catwalk on either side. Past that, the shaft narrowed ominously as it climbed uphill again, growing tight enough that he was scraping the walls on both sides and had to sidle along at an angle with his head awkwardly low to keep from banging it on the rough block and mortar.

No wonder it was not well traveled. A misstep here would send him sprawling into the slimy cesspit below.

A set of rough stairs appeared ahead at the end of the line, for the tunnel was becoming too narrow to pass. The faint haze of CG came with a glimmer of green daylight, so he put his torch away and safety checked his mask and goggles. The steps came out in a basement below a knackery, and he hustled up them, trying not to think too much of the nasty things that had floated past him. He popped out of a coal chute, covered with cobwebs and dark dust.

The street was quiet, nothing had opened for business yet, though he ducked back as someone on the other side stepped out briefly in a mask and robe to empty a chamber pot into the gutter. On either side of the building he scrambled out of was a butcher and a tanner—that explained the filth! It had to the low end of the mercantile district, likely Drury Lane. Quite a ways from Wintersmith's Palace, but it would give him time to plan and gather the materials he needed.

Simon was not content to leaving Mattie to her fate, as the Mayweathers had left him. She had come to warn him, and got herself captured. If she lived, he'd get her out of there.

***

Queen Anne Eliza Wintersmith was a striking woman, as chillingly lovely to gaze upon as a glacier, and just as cold and unyielding. She had all the regal, imperious personage of someone born to nobility, and yet, the scar on her left cheek spoke of a somewhat more humble and far less titled origin. She was someone to be reckoned with, for Anne Wintersmith had battled her way to the top—both figuratively and literally—and she was not about to let anyone interfere with her plans to dominate first New Southampton, and then whatever was left of civilization around it.

She was well aware of an undercurrent of insurgents seeking to usurp her authority, though at first she had given them no mind. The Mayweathers were vexing enough, but not many citizens sympathized with them; their preaching was barmy at best, and their methods brutal and non-selective. Recently though, more personable and endearing cavalier groups had emerged on the scene, and they were capturing the hearts and minds of the rabble, as well as some of the gullible middle class. Wintersmith despised them all; these bourgeois benevolent heroes of the street—especially those freaks of the Crater Holocaust area popularly known as "Gassers".

Their mutated forms she found disconcerting to gaze upon, and since most of them became either beggars or thieves, they added no coin to the coffers. If they were suffered to live at all, they would either be brought under the yoke of the realm, or they'd be broken on its appurtenances. For all her lofty position, she was a savvy woman who kept an ear to cobbled streets, and so she knew which of those outlaw rebels living below polite society were most admired. Those she targeted especially with a series of lightning raids meant to show the Great Unwashed that such foolishly romantic notions of sedition would be dealt with swiftly and severely. It also served as a warning to keep any would-be dissidents amongst her cabinet and court on their toes, for treason was a capital offense, and public executions were becoming far more commonplace. "Bloody Annie", as they referred to her in the marketplace and residential sections, was ruthless; and her Regulators of Discord were everywhere.

She was dressed today in her official surcoat of red wool with black frog fasteners, over a black silk taffeta dress for which just the material cost in this backward age would feed a destitute family for a year. Anne Wintersmith never gave that a second thought as her lady maid finished with an elaborately arranged upsweep of her dark hair. Society had its classes and there would always be poor.

She rose gracefully from her dressing room chair and gazed in the mirror. Deep set, kohl rimmed green eyes that could seem stormy gray in some lights scanned her image from head to toe with frank candor. With her high cheekbones rouged and lightly painted bow lips compressed into a very tight and deadly smile, she appeared dignified, and uncompromising. Perfect!

"That will do; you are dismissed," she said firmly in a voice that was low and rich in timbre. "Tell my chamberlain to have Major Aldridge meet me on the way down." She swept from the room without a backward glance, knowing that the foursome of well armed guards would automatically arrange themselves before and behind her. There were things a queen could take for granted if she ruled with an iron fist in a velvet glove, and a steel trap mind.

Halfway to her goal, the men ahead parted as Reginald Aldridge fell into step beside her. They were given a respectable distance so that they might converse in low tones without being overheard.

"Your Majesty," the tall, straight-backed man said with a deferential bow. "I came as soon as I could get away–"

She waved him to silence. "Yes, yes Reginald. I'm not big on formalities between busy compatriots, so let us cut to the chase here. Who is it that we have nabbed this time? I hope you're going to tell me this is that elusive being known as The Rebel! I'd so love to see that one strung up."

He sighed, and shook his head. "I wish I could, but unfortunately, the answer is no. The Rebel works alone, and as we've discussed before, the solitary criminal is the most elusive. However, we did manage to tease out one of the bigger thorns in the wild hedge," he said with unusual good cheer. "Mattie Fox has been quite successful as both a common thief and lately a spy. We have reason to believe she has strong ties with other rebel factions. Our sources tell us she's lifted some very important documents and done quite a bit of street recruiting too."

"So we have quite the prize indeed. What are we presently doing with her?" Wintersmith asked curiously as they rounded a corner and entered a steam powered lift that would take them down to the lowest levels.

"Nothing so far," he said apologetically. "We'd just barely gotten her installed this morning. She's in the solitary confinement cell. I thought you'd want to see her before we begin the interrogation."

"She's a Gasser then?" Wintersmith asked, turning her green eyes up to meet his.

He nodded gravely. "Yes, caught in a raid just outside of the market. We took a few other prisoners last night, but no one as notable. She was turned over by that bounty hunter, Kirkland. He caught her coming through a building wall."

That got him a raised eyebrow and a speculative look. "Interesting. And she's well known to the general populace?"

"Quite," he assured her.

"Yes, I do want to view her first. We'll do whatever we must to get some information out of her, but I'd prefer keep her intact for now. We'll have a public execution and see if we can flush out a few more of their kind in the process. I don't want her in such pitiable shape that she garners audience sympathy or proves useless to our researchers."

As the lift hit the bottom and the door was cranked open, already the wheels were turning in Wintersmith's devious mind.

***

A couple hours of shuteye and then some discrete inquiries had verified Mattie Fox had been taken into custody last night and the gaol wagon had taken her to the palace grounds and not the Eastleigh garrison. That made things more complicated. Word on the street was, they had a new dungeon there, with some very old, tried-and-true methods of coercion.

It didn't matter. Mattie was as close as he'd ever had to a friend. He tugged at a loose board beneath the bed in his one room rental flop, and, swinging it aside, reached in to pull out the former tools of his trade with the Mayweathers, the tool belt and bracers that had little pockets for various items. They were all still there, along with the hand drawn maps. He grabbed the one that interested him most—the schematic to Wintersmith's Palace—and studied it by the light of a single candle.

With a modicum of planning, it could be done...

Simon had geared up and was heading out that night when one of Morgan Mather's strong arms stopped him. This man was a miniature mountain, just under six feet and seventeen stone, most of it muscle.

"Ye'd best be on yer way ta Claremont Street. Boss says you dinna finish the job," he said, grabbing Simon's arm.

Simon pulled away irritably. "There was a raid, Scully. If I got taken, I'd not have finished the job anyway."

"See that ya do, or ye'll not git paid," the bigger man said. "If ya think the Reggies will be tough to avoid, ya don' wanna be spendin' yer night's dodging me." The brass knuckles attached to his gloved bracers were infamous for breaking noses and jawbones and cracking a few skulls as well.

"Just tell Morgan I'm on it," Simon said and edged away in the opposite direction he wanted to go. He didn't like that they knew where he lived.

***

Queen Anne had asked that the gas be redirected so that she could view Mattie Fox through the thick porthole. "She isn't very impressive," she said frankly to Major Aldridge. They stood alone together in the observation area, the Regulator guards that always hovered around the queen having been dismissed to wait just outside the door, where they kept anyone from entering without express permissions from within.

"I assure you, she's been quite effective," Aldridge said with distaste. "She's canny and fast and led us on many a merry chase. *We* can't pass through solid walls, but obviously she can. I don't think Kirkland would have located her without those goggles."

Wintersmith smiled thinly but triumphantly. "So my investment paid off. I told you that dissecting these creatures," she indicated Mattie crouched in the cell below them warily, with a sweep of a hand, "would do us some good. That particular mechanical advance came from one of the crater gassers we killed. It had been attacking troopers in the dark—because it could actually see them. When they took its eyes apart, our scientists were able to fabricate something similar with lenses and other materials. We must remind Kirkland that device is to be returned once he's paid."

"You may be assured I will see to that," Aldridge countered. "I'm curious though, why haven't we started the questioning process with her?"

She turned eyes up to him and ran an arm through his at the elbow, patting his hand with hers. "Patience Reginald! I have a plan in motion; one that will secure us a full confession and still leave a prisoner with a well-tended appearance to parade at the execution tomorrow with a body we can analyze later. You will momentarily see what cunning the wolf has when the fox is trapped in her lair." A white wolf's head with teeth bared had been Wintersmith's heraldic symbol through her rise to power.

A cautious knock came. The queen stepped away from Aldridge and bid whoever it was to enter. The guard bowed deeply. "All is prepared, My Liege," he said.

"Very good!" She turned back to Aldridge while checking the gear wound chronometer attached to one of her court bracers. "You're invited to observe at the inquest if you choose," she told him before she swept past and her men gathered around her. "I can promise it will be quite enlightening."

***

Mattie watched carefully through the backlit observation window. There were two figures silhouetted against the glass. One was definitely the queen; there was no mistaking her monarchical bearing. The other was a tall man she'd never encountered before. They seemed quite chummy, almost affectionate. No surprise there; gossip all over the city said Wintersmith had several lovers, and kept them all dancing in attendance.

They left the viewing room, and within moments the CG flowed back over the window again. There must be some sort of valve system that allowed them to cut it off in that one spot. That might be useful information should she have a chance to make a break for it, though no doubt the area outside her cell was well guarded. She had no illusions winning her freedom, because unless she managed to escape on her own, she'd hang on the morrow.

Within minutes her enclosure was being reeled up. Mattie was a bit surprised they had not dealt with her sooner. She'd soon find out if her outlaw reputation had grown enough to warrant Her Majesty bearing witness to her interrogation.

Time for my curtain call!

When the ascent stopped, there was the squeaking sound of the hand wheel being turned, and then a light came through the opened hatch. A guard had his hand cannon trained on her.

"Get out here, you!" he said, motioning her to step over the lip. "Her Majesty is a'waitin' to watch you scream out your confession!" He laughed wickedly.

Mattie was apprehensive, but remained cool-headed. She'd been in tight spots before. She screwed up her nerve, and said lightly, "Well, an audience with the queen! I'm honored."

Another man moved behind her to tie back her aching arms. She considered making a break for it then but decided against it, for the one before her still had the weapon trained on her. He couldn't miss at that range, and there were guards all around. While it might be better to die cleanly rather than writhing in pain hours later, Mattie was an optimist by nature.

I'll find some way out of this.

They yanked her along by the leash of plastique, marching her smartly to the room with the inquest table. Mattie stood blinking in the now unaccustomed light. Before her sat Bloody Annie; all prim, icy elegance. A high ranking military official was seated to her right, the rotund and balding head gaoler to her left, and a bewigged judge beside him. They were surrounded by a contingent of well armed guards.

Mattie was a little confused when they attached her shackling line to a wall behind her, and then dragged in another prisoner. A ragged young man, likely only a pickpocket from the looks of him, barely past the age of voice change. He was firmly tied to a rough wooden chair. Big, scared eyes in a bruised face full of dread looked around fearfully.

They set the chair with the struggling prisoner before her, and then wheeled up a brazier full of glowing coals. Several iron pokers were shoved within to heat, and her heart dropped. A man of authority arrived, his red vestments and peaked cap pronouncing him one of the interrogation team. He bowed to the Queen.

"You may begin, Lucian," Wintersmith said in a voice without warmth. He nodded with a slight smile, and turned on a heel to pace before Mattie, his lips curled like a cat watching a mouse under its paw.

"I present to you, the notorious Mattie Fox!" he said as if introducing the next act in a side show.

"All this circus, and me just a common thief!" she said with calculated disrespect. "I must be comin' up in the world." Mattie was stalling for time, because she didn't want those hot irons used on anyone—especially someone who didn't deserve it. The poor lad was a petty thief as best, and looked as if he hadn't eaten well or often.

A rough hand from one of her gaolers snapped her head sideways, loosening a tooth. She bit her lip hard and it bled. Her left cheek swelled up purple, making her eye squint. "No speaking out of turn!" she was warned.

The queen looked unhappy, and she leaned in toward the head gaoler, who lumbered to his feet.

"Do not manhandle the prisoner being questioned—Her Majesty's orders!" he said in his squeaky voice. "Now proceed."

"Matilda Foxborough," began the inquisitor again in his stentorian voice as his men donned thick, fireproof gloves, "More popularly known as Mattie Fox. Besides your rather checkered past, we have reason to believe you have forged alliances with revolutionary enemies of the realm. That is treason. The penalty for treason is death by hanging. Your fate is foreordained."

"Yeah, so why should I tell you anything if I'm going to die anyway?" Mattie retorted with an insolent look, trying to bring their attention back on her and off the quaking lad.

"For mercy's sake; if you have any left in your renegade soul," Lucian the Inquisitor said with an edge to his voice. He was furious with her flippant attitude, itching to make her scream out what they wanted to know and be done with it. "If you are cooperative, and give us the information we need, this other young miscreant," he flicked a manicured finger at the quailing youth, "will not suffer any further harm at your expense. If not…" he paused dramatically and nodded at one of his men to pull a red hot branding iron from the embers, "he's going to have a very difficult time getting comfortable in his cell tonight."

"Bugger off!" she said, hoping they were bluffing, or that her attitude would change their minds and they'd torture her instead.

Lucian nodded and the man walked over. He dispassionately applied the hot iron to the lad's downy cheek for just a moment while another held his head steady. The screech of agony was deafening as his body writhed within the bonds. Tears ran down the boy's face after the brand was pulled away. The reddened skin blistered immediately. Head lolling with the pain, he sobbed pitifully.

"Oh gods, don't do that to him!" Mattie begged. "He's nothing to do with me and mine." She glared at the Queen but the woman sat expressionless, her elegant hands full of rings folded before her on the table.

"Then tell us what we need to know, Matilda, or I shall have to punish him again on your behalf," Lucian the Inquisitor said. "Where is the entrance to the rebel base?" he began. When she was slow to respond, he motioned for another iron to be pulled. "I'm running out of patience," he warned her in a mock teasing tone as the second man crossed to where the boy sat squirming in terror.

Do I betray my friends or do I let this boy suffer?

"Under the monorail station at Fareham," she said quickly. It was a little used back exit. They could easily block it off.

The iron was replaced in the brazier.

"Now we're getting somewhere," Lucian said. "Who are their principal members?"

Mattie's reluctant answers were the only thing preventing the searing agony of a boy she didn't know.

***

He had to watch his step; it was dark and there was slag rubble all over the place from the new wall going up. Simon scuttled along in the shadows and set his first charge at the base of the temporary guard tower on the east side. He had to lay low for many tense moments while a couple men strode up and climbed the ladder, passing no more than inches from where he hid. He lit the long fuse, and moved on.

The plan was simple and hinged on the fact that he knew the

general layout of the palace from maps he had seen during his Mayweather days. A small blasting stick with a long fuse—easily enough purchased on the street if you knew whom to ask—would make a suitable amount of noise and rubble, crumpling the tower with low chance of innocent casualties. If all went well, it should completely distract the exterior guards. A second one set to go off a while later should stop a very important cogged wheel in the pump house that adjoined the boiler. Panic should prevail then, as the same power source that allowed interior illumination also kept out the CG.

Panic, Simon knew from his past experiences, was the insurgent's best weapon. While the Regulators were sending men out to investigate, Simon would free Mattie. He had a sketchy idea of where she would be in the deep cellars beneath the old town hall building, and the dungeon placement suggested some east end postern entrance. It made no sense to go in that way, which would be the most heavily guarded. There had to be access from elsewhere in the palace or the building beneath, and that's what Simon meant to find as he slipped over an unoccupied section of north curtain wall, which was still under construction.

The bulk of the gallows rising above the wall facing the marketplace was a mute and sinister reminder that the clock was ticking. Word on the street was the execution was scheduled for mid-morning, when people would be out and about. Mattie would be most accessible then, but that's also when the Regulators would be expecting any sort of rescue attempt. He had to reach her now.

Drawing near to where the iron palace's five stories squatted atop the older building, Simon could see that getting inside and out again was going to be far trickier than he had thought. Once the second bomb went off, all levels would be closed off and crawling with Reggies. Hopefully they wouldn't realize immediately that it was a cover for something else!

He dropped down noiselessly to the rough ground below, remaining in a crouch until a small contingent of guards escorting a priest passed by. Wintersmith was noted for currying favor with the church. They were headed toward the back of the palace, so Simon shadowed them, staying low and darting rapidly across the better lit areas, praying he would not be seen in the half gloom of the CG. They might be offering the condemned a chance at absolution. Wherever they were going, he would have his best chance at getting inside.

Adrenaline fueled by anxiety and excitement put his abnormal nervous system on high alert. As he dodged from pillar to post, statue to fountain, the changes in his outward pattern came so rapidly his skin prickled and itched. He'd not felt such intense fear since living with the Mayweathers, where every raid was all but guaranteed to result in deaths. Yet what he had learned from them now served him well.

The service ingress ramp that the priest's group headed into was lightly guarded. A carefully tossed chunk of slag made the single sentry move around the corner to see what had fallen. Blending in with the walls and shadows, Simon was able to slip past and inside. He skulked just behind the priest and his party as they went on, noiselessly following their descent.

The first bomb went off then and drew the majority of guards away from where the second one had been planted on the pump house roof.

The men he followed turned abruptly left after the first set of stairs downward. That was the wrong direction. It was not the dungeon level as he had hoped for, and Simon lost them when the sound of dragging footsteps and something rumbling along echoed down a cross hall. Flattening against a wall, he narrowly avoided a drudge who was rolling an empty barrel.

There must be a wine cellar nearby. That gave Simon an idea. He followed the servant, taking up a bung mallet on the way. A carefully executed rap on the temple, and the wretched fool crumpled like a rag doll. Simon grabbed the inexpensive one piece mask in the bag on his belt, and added it to his own. No doubt Mattie would not have been allowed to keep her rig, and she'd need something outside. Executions being fatal affairs, prisoners were taken to the gallows bareheaded.

Grabbing a small cask of expensive brandy, he levered the bung with his knife and added the contents of a tiny bottle pulled from his belt along with a short length of fuse. He tapped the bung back in place, hefted it and moved toward the next set of stairs, heading down in the general direction of the dungeon.

There were two archways at the bottom, and the first time he took the wrong one and wound up trapped in a storage area while a couple men loitered outside. They were talking about prisoners they had dealt with that day, laughing and slapping each other on the back as choice details of the punishments were shared. He touched the comforting grip of his stiletto, but Simon kept his head about him and eventually they moved on. He had lost significant time to their lollygagging, but he surmised by their jovial camaraderie they were just recently off duty. That meant the dungeon was in the direction they had just come from.

The place was a maze of archways and a beehive of activity. Many times he had to flatten himself against rock or dart around a corner as someone passed nearby.

He was just in time to see a glowing brazier being wheeled through the next arch. There were several guards standing nearby; watching the "fun" he supposed. Simon had to find a way around them. A man's voice droned on and there was some sort of an answer, and then the a sizzle and the sounds of a youngster howling. The guards ahead had a low voiced conversation. One kept snickering, while others snapped at him that the queen would have his head on a platter if he kept being so loud.

This was the sort of tyrannical climate Wintersmith was breeding, class warfare within a strict and unforgiving autocracy. In that respect the Mayweathers had interpreted her regime perfectly, Simon realized with a shudder. Unfortunately, their methods of fighting back were far too brutally similar.

As Simon crept closer, he could see little but was able to hear the inquisitor's demanding questions over the sobbing of the other prisoner, with Mattie's halting answers in flat tones afterward. The dirty fiends were using her sympathy for her fellow inmate to get what information they could from her!

The next question came just before a muffled explosion across the complex rocked the building above. The gas lights flickered and then went out and people began shouting. The guards in front of Simon ran off to investigate, moving past where he was huddled in the shadows, barely daring to breathe.

Grit and dust sifted down from the vaulted arches overhead and the pipes rattled when the pressure pump went on and off. People began to shout fearfully that the CG would begin filtering in as they opened emergency cabinets or tugged on personal masks. There was brief, loud discussion about the backup system, and the room began to empty.

Men were coming his way. They might not see him, but the brandy cask was not part of his normal gear. In desperation, he sat down on it, willing his body blend in with the wall and floor. For a few tense moments Simon held his breath as people strode within inches of his hiding place.

The steam whistles were not working, but someone had dragged out the old hand crank air raid warning siren, and it began wailing away like a million alley cats. Feet were pounding all around Simon as he slid into the deepest shadows. The backup pressure system faltered and went down completely. Someone insisted the queen needed to be taken to safety. Someone else was bellowing that the prisoners had to be secured.

He warily regained his feet and took a cautious peek into the chamber. His eyes rounded at the sight of Queen Anne in the half-darkness, limned with ruddy firelight and looking quite the part of the demoness she was reputed to be. She was standing behind a table where she had just been sitting, pointing and barking orders, her eyes wild and glittering from the glow of the brazier, on which someone had thrown more wood. A tall man with a hand cannon was tugging at her Ladyship's arm, urging her to put on her mask and leave. Men ran about in confusion, bumping into each other in the darker areas while attempting to secure the prisoners. Several manhandled a cringing young man tied to a chair. Simon saw the scared eyes of the youth and his blistered cheek as they hauled him away, and his heart went out to the lad. They'd leave him to choke to death down here with all the rest.

Now was his best chance to save Mattie. Simon yanked on his own mask and goggles, turning the lenses to dark sight. He picked up the brandy cask, and slunk into chamber. In the flickering gloom, two guards were tugging Mattie off to her isolation cell. He heaved the cask into the brazier. It hit with a resounding thunk and slosh, knocking it over onto the floor, where the chemical he added to the alcohol produced a prodigious and dazzling fireball. Blue and yellow flames spread along the rushes and trash on the floor.

Simon faded into the darkness behind Mattie as the remaining people ran in all directions; some to escape and others to find something to beat out the spreading flames. A tap on the shoulder and then a quick uppercut to the chin took out the guard closest to her. She seized the opportunity to kick the other one square in the bawbles, and when the man went over cursing and groaning, brought her arms around to knock him face down. His head and nose hit the rock floor rather hard. He would not be getting up for a while.

"What are you doing here?" she said with her arms outthrust as Simon pulled his blade and sawed through her bonds. She rubbed her wrists, getting the circulation back.

"We'll talk later," he told her brusquely, before handing her the extra mask. The CG hadn't seeped down there yet, but if the pumps were badly damaged, they would run into it in the upper levels. They grabbed the weapons of the two guards, and Simon gave each one an extra wallop behind the ear with a wooden grip before tucking a pistol into his belt. "Let's get the devil out of here before someone discovers you're not in your cell."

"What's the best route?" she asked as he motioned her to follow behind him in the dark.

"Back up to the wine cellar level, because there's plenty of room to hide until some of this panic blows over. We've got a lot of ground to cover and this place is crawling with Regulators."

"You let me worry about them," Mattie said with determination. "This part of the building is stone and I've little problem with that. I just can't walk outside and take a chance that someone will be waiting for us—and I can't take you through a wall with me either, Love," she reminded him.

"I'll think of something," he promised her. He still had a few tricks left unused and the thought of the boy dying down here for Mattie's sake was haunting him. Simon recalled all too well what it was like to be left for dead.

His first duty though was to get Mattie to freedom.

They stayed away from the upper, inhabited areas of the building and headed toward the back, trying to find a way out. It was a harrowing couple of hours as they played cat and mouse with Regulator groups. Simon insisted they be economical with the pistols, since they were noisy and there was no way to reload. As soon as anyone came their way, they split up, with him hiding while Mattie went through a wall to get ahead. She'd lead the chase onward, turn a corner, and disappear into a wall while Simon either took out the pursuers or simply moved on. A couple times they were almost captured when someone else came up quickly from behind. Shots whistled by their heads and ricocheted nearby, chipping the stone as they ran for their lives.

Unfortunately the wine cellar was blocked by an entire squad, all well armed. They retreated back the way they came, but there was someone coming up the stairs behind them now and the sound of voices drifted down from above.

"I might win free, but you're trapped in here," she whispered. The CG had finally started to filter in, wisps of it twisting past them like viridian wraiths.

"I've got an idea. Distract him for me," Simon hissed, having decided to take his chances with the single guard. She melted into the wall as he flattened himself into a shadowy niche at one side of the head of the stairs. The man was halfway up when Mattie appeared below and behind him.

"Looking for me, Ducks?" she asked in a quiet voice, and stood tauntingly in view, hands on hips. Her opponent drew his weapon and spun around, but that's all he had time for when Simon landed on him. He had angled his jump to knock the pistol loose and it skittered away while they rolled around on the floor, grunting and trading blows.

The Reggie was about his size but more compactly muscled than wiry Simon. Simon knew he was outclassed in both strength and training, but wily desperation born of far too many brutal encounters in his life gave him just enough of an edge. As far back as he could recall, he had been wrestling and sparring with his Mayweather "brothers and sisters"—most of which were viciously effective in thuggery of the most bestial variety. He had learned early to vigorously defend himself or he never would have had enough to eat and a dry place to sleep.

That all came back in a rush and before the hapless guard could reach for his knife, Simon had him pinned and was slugging him relentlessly when Mattie came up and simply conked him in the head with his own weapon. The guard crumpled into a heap and lay very still.

"I had him," Simon said through gritted teeth, getting off the now prone figure.

"You were both making too much noise," she whispered back and gestured. "Someone else might happen along or that lot above have heard you." She shoved the second weapon in her belt. "What are we going to do with him?"

"I'll show you," he said grabbing the unconscious man's legs while Mattie took his arms. They dragged him out of sight, quickly stripping and tying him with his own belt before gagging him with his small clothes. Simon refused to use the guard's own manacles on him. They put Mattie's cheap mask over his head, and covered him with Simon's cape. Simon struggled into the Regulator's suit, which was a bit baggy on him. He used his own belt to cinch it, hoping in the darkness and confusion, no one would notice, and pulled on the regulation mask while Mattie donned his.

"I take the weapons," he whispered. He picked up a conventional pair of manacles the guard had been carrying. "I'm sorry, but you have to wear these."

"Why bother?" she asked, frowning but turning so he could fasten them behind her back. "I can slip those easily enough."

"That's the point," he said grimly. "Let's hope the rest don't know that, because right now you're our ticket out of here. I'm transporting a rebel leader for questioning. You'll have to convince them you've been done down, but be on your toes. If you get a chance to make a break for it, just go. When we split up we'll be harder to find."

"It could work..." Mattie said doubtfully as they ascended the stairs again toward the service entrance. "What about you?"

"Once you're off, I'll give them more to think about," Simon said cryptically, but didn't explain. He wasn't quite sure yet what he actually meant to do, but having gotten a glimpse of the poor lad who had been branded on Mattie's behalf, he wondered how many other minor miscreants had been incarcerated in that hell-hole. Something had stirred inside him this day; something more than being simply Simon, the Gasser who had fled the Mayweathers to eke out an existence as a minor underworld enforcer.

Perhaps there was another way to make a difference—a path less violent and more honorable, yet made use of his natural talent for stealth.

Simon turned his life in a new direction that day.

***

The commander of the palace's night watch saluted smartly in the CG gloom. "Status report!" Wintersmith barked through her mask. She and her personal guards were standing in the south side cupola, where she had been watching the activity below.

"The temporary tower on the east side and part of the new wall behind it went down." the man began in a voice filled with trepidation. "Another blast went off on the pump house a short while later, and I'm afraid that's going to be a lengthy repair. We have two troopers dead and twenty injured—most not seriously, though several inside got a good lungful of gas. Some of the maintenance workers are still trapped inside the building–"

She cut him off. "I don't have the patience to listen to bellyaching about who was injured—count and care for them on your own time. Your first and foremost task is to find whoever dared do this!" she demanded, seething that someone had actually gotten that far inside the grounds. "I want all the miscreants involved rounded up by sunrise, for I intend to see them executed before the day is out."

"As you command, Your Grace," the man said shakily. He dipped his head in deference.

"See to it immediately or you and your officers will take their place. Dismissed," she added, waving him off without further comment. One of her personal retinue escorted the now thoroughly intimidated man to the stairs while Wintersmith turned back to viewing the grounds below, her back ramrod straight and lips compressed in a grimace of displeasure. At Reginald Aldridge's insistence, her private airship was moored above and waiting to whisk her off, should this turn out to be a coup attempt. She would only avail herself of that if things escalated.

The entire night had been a disaster! Besides the two explosions, which were going to be costly, the high profile prisoner had somehow escaped during the confusion and was loose in the warrens below. Aldridge was working on that, but the Gasser's talent made her hard to track. If she escaped, word would spread quickly amongst the commoners, and they'd have another hero to applaud.

Rumor had it the Mayweathers had attacked—blasting sticks were their forte. Wintersmith didn't think so, but allowing the rabble to believe that would help her save face. Few loved Cyrus' revolutionary movement, for he spared no one in his blind zeal.

Let them have their small victory then. Her army was growing, and they would continue to root out these rebel units. More Gassers would be put down like the curs that they were. Still, anyone with a penchant for adventure and a bone to pick with the crown would see this escape as a call to join the movement, and the rest of the rabble would cheer them on. That lead to insurrection, and if they united under one banner, a general revolt.

We'll crush them first! I have not yet unleashed the full spectrum of my system.

***

The group on the floor above them had dispersed, and only three had been left to guard the entrance. Better odds, that was. Two were well armed Regulators, and not inclined to let even one of their own pass unchallenged. The third was a female Evol, which made things complicated.

"Prisoner transport," Simon announced in a guttural voice beneath his mask while keeping his distance. Mattie sagged convincingly in his grasp, shambling long with one foot tangling around the other like some drunken lout.

"Let me see your papers," prompted the Reggie who seemed to be the normal checkpoint guard. He thrust a gloved hand out. The other Reggie glanced back briefly; he had the insignia of a sergeant. He stood just outside the doorway, talking low with the Evol, who was scanning the yard. She was tall and well muscled, and would not be easily overcome, even if they did manage to take out the other two.

"Uh… I don't have any," Simon said. "I was just ordered to get her out of there."

"No one comes or goes without an official writ—Aldridge's orders," the checkpoint guard insisted. He kept his hand on his pistol and his eyes on Mattie, who feigned being docile and barely conscious.

Simon began pleading his case. "Look, we all thought the building was coming down on us. It was chaos, and there was no time to find a superior. If this one gets away, Her Royal..." he almost said "Pain In the Arse", "Her *Majesty* is going to have all our heads on pikes.

"Until I see a signature, you don't pass," the checkpoint guard restated firmly.

"We can't go back, there was a fire down there," Simon argued, sweeping an arm behind him to indicate the dungeon area. "We were told to remove the important prisoners who might help us find the rebel bases." He pulled Mattie's mask back just far enough so the man could see her bruised cheek. "They were in the midst of questioning this one when the alarms sounded. Her Majesty wants to find out what else these traitors are up to."

"What nonsense is this?" The sergeant had stepped back inside. His stance said he was suspicious and expected trouble.

Simon began to sweat inside the double layers of leather and cloth. They weren't buying it!

"I have to get her to the tower to continue questioning before something else blows up."

"Oh really; and just what would that be, trooper?" the sergeant said, noting Simon's ill fitting uniform. He took a step forward with his pistol now drawn. "Where did you get that belt? That's not regulation issue."

"Sir, it was dark down there and I was off duty. When the sirens went off, I grabbed whatever I could find."

"Is that why you have Corporal Sedgewicke's uniform on?" Simon groaned inwardly. This sergeant knew his badge numbers.

The Evol had half turned toward them and she began to stalk sinuously in their direction. The sergeant waved her off, but she persisted. "There is someone unnatural here," the Evol declared in a precise tone.

It was time to make a move.

"Yeah, she's a Gasser. Fine then, you deal with this guttersnipe. I've better things to do," Simon didn't think they'd shoot Mattie, so he shoved her at the sergeant, effectively blocking his gun, before quickly retreating back the way he'd come. He hoped she would forgive him, but she was on her own now.

Mattie landed bonelessly in the sergeant's arms, and got roughly shoved aside. "Bring that insolent prig back to me," the sergeant ordered the other two men as he holstered his sidearm. "If he's one of us, I'll have him stripped of his uniform and demoted to city patrol."

The Evol and checkpoint guard raced after Simon. The sergeant turned back to Mattie just in time to see her disappear through the wall. Her manacles lay neatly nearby, and when he went to draw it, his pistol was gone. A hand groped around his neck, and found the light-fingered lass had taken his whistle as well.

"Aldridge will have my badge for this," he groaned before pulling the rope that rang the warning bell summoning the nearest grounds sweep patrol.

***

Later it would be reported that while an attack by Mayweather terrorists was going on, a prisoner scheduled to be executed managed to overpower her guards and escaped, setting a few other prisoners free. The official state declaration was that they were all successfully captured and executed privately.

The truth was something else altogether…

The elusive Mattie Fox disappeared into the green gloom of the back streets that favored those whose business was unlawful. Posters with crude etchings of her were put up all over New Southampton, as well as on the monorail. They were given to all airship and steamship captains, and of course to the fugitive hunters, who were promised specialized goggles if they signed an exclusive contract with the crown.

There had been a mass escape amongst the Gassers and suspected rebel alliance members being held in the dungeon. Some were recaptured and executed, a few died fighting for their freedom, but that day, the majority of the men, women, and youngsters languishing in Wintersmith's new dungeon were given their freedom by a mysterious man who told them where to find masks and weapons, and then shed a Regulator outfit with the help of a long stiletto. When they asked him who he was, he answered simply, "I'm Simon," before he disappeared into the night.

Simon Simple gained a lot of friends and admirers that night. He would never have to fear being turned into the Mayweathers again.

THE REBEL

by
Lee Houston Jr.

Personal Log: 3 January, 2075

As I take quill to parchment and my homeland enters its fifth year of autocratic sovereignty, I find myself increasingly conflicted between duty and honor. My loyalties divided twixt crown and country.

On one hand, "Queen" Anne Eliza Wintersmith is far from the rightful ruler of New Southampton. Yet her despotic reign is better than the anarchy that would arise if the Mayweather Guardians of Normality or one of the other groups that plague our fair city are ever victorious.

Many, like myself, continue to silently pray that someday Doctor Fulbright will return to us alive and well. Most citizens consider New Southampton's founder our savior, for true Humans were a war ravaged race with little hope of survival before he came forth to help. It would come as no surprise to me if Wintersmith fears an uprising to make Fulbright King upon his return.

And if she should discover my involvement in the events that plague her unrightful time in power…

***

Nights within the walled boundaries of New Southampton are similar to its days, regardless of which district one might find themselves in. The Creeping Green is ever present. Thicker than the densest fog of old and far more hazardous, a constant reminder of what we have lost and the uncertainty of our future. Yet there is a uniqueness to the darkness. A sense of hope hiding within the cold miasma. That things will be better with the coming dawn, despite the fact that only a privileged few will witness the sunrise.

In the distance, I heard the bells of St. George's Chapel solemnly chime three. The clockworks within its steeple automatically struck the hour, for all good parishioners should be in bed asleep. However there were demons amongst the angels, and I could not allow myself the luxury of rest until all under my protection were safe.

Thanks to the current configuration of the special lenses within my goggles, I spotted her through the emerald mist with clarity, as if it was an ancient, bright sunny day. Approaching from the side street was a woman I knew. Poor Mary Margaret, nothing more than a severely overworked and grossly underpaid kitchen servant within the Iron Palace, was trying to race back to her family in the hovel they call home. The only thing upon her mind at that moment was the hope of catching a few precious hours of sleep amongst her loved ones before having to return and serve "Her Royal Highness" once more cometh the dawn.

Unfortunately there was no time to intercept her, because from another angle of my rooftop perch, I spotted two members of Queen Wintersmith's very misnamed Regulators of Discord out on patrol. This group was supposed to help guard the city from all that plagues it. However they often sowed more conflict than they controlled, depending upon Wintersmith's moods and plans, for who regulated the Regulators?

I watched these two specimens of royal law enforcement stroll down the cobblestone sidewalk, for not every patrol was assigned transportation. Most of the back alleys in the poorer areas were too narrow for even a monowheel to traverse, so the steam powered velocipedes were used in the more affluent sections of the city to present added intimidation to the criminal element there. In truth, the Crown looked out for its supporters more than the common folks.

As the players drew closer to the gas lamp on the corner, the stage was set. I silently moved along the rooftops to await my cue in the drama unfolding below me.

***

"Well, well. What do we have here?" one Regulator asked the other, while grabbing Mary Margaret by her left arm as she tried to cross the street in front of them. Every mask was designed to allow normal breathing within the Creeping Green without hindering communication, even between vermin.

"Please good sirs, I want no trouble," pleaded the innocent woman. "I have my papers right here," she said, attempting to reach with her free hand into the pocket of the soiled apron around her waist.

"What are you doing out past curfew?" the first Regulator demanded to know as he grabbed Mary Margaret's other arm. He held them roughly behind her back, giving no thought of how much this action might hurt the kitchen servant.

Meanwhile, his partner removed and started going through everything from the apron pocket. From overhead, I couldn't tell whether or not the man did anything to take advantage of the situation, for Mary Margaret's voice was already showing signs of distress.

"The Queen held a grand dinner party tonight for the gentry and I had to work late," explained the woman in a frightened tone. "I have a note from the Master of the Kitchen himself, granting me permission to go home now so I can check on my children, despite the curfew."

I hoped her offspring could look after themselves. I knew Mary Margaret's husband toiled long hours within the Wintersmith Ironworks, but never realized he might not be home right now.

"What do you think Bill?" asked the first Regulator.

"Well Len, there *is* a note here, on official looking stationery and everything," the other man replied, while briefly holding up the document for his companion to see. "But it could be a forgery," he added, before crumbling the certificate up and stuffing it into a pants pocket.

"That's what I was thinking," replied Len, as both men stared at Mary Margaret. "This little strumpet could actually be out plying her *true* trade." While the realm issued mask obscured most of her face and servants' clothing was far from flattering, there was no hiding the feminine curves of the middle aged woman.

"But by the Queen's commands, that's illegal too," said Bill, in a mock state of shock.

"I suppose if we teach this harlot the error of her ways, maybe we can let her off with just a warning this time," suggested Len, as he pulled Mary Margaret closer to his body and began to run his hands up toward her ample bosom.

That was when I took action. Jumping off the roof cornice above, I brought my full weight to bear and landed squarely upon Bill, feet first.

My sudden appearance accomplished everything I had hoped for. Although it was only a two story fall, Bill collapsed upon the cobblestones below us with a resounding "thunk", thus rendering him at least stunned, if not completely unconscious.

Meanwhile, with his full attention now upon me, Len let go of his intended victim as he started to draw his sword from its sheath. This allowed Mary Margaret to hastily grab her other papers from the sidewalk where they laid next to the fallen Regulator. Then she ran for home as fast as she could, while my gloved right hand drew my father's sword from its scabbard. Despite being the youngest of three, his cherished weapon came to me upon his passing because my brothers are still missing in action.

"I may have missed out on some tasty pleasure this night, but capturing The Rebel will more than make up for a lost romp," boasted Len as our swords clashed.

My opponent's fighting skills were practically nonexistent. What he lacked in tactics, style, and finesse, Len over compensated for with brute strength and dirty tricks. As I easily parried every swipe of his blade, the Regulator tried punching or kicking me whenever the opportunity presented itself. Most of those blows I was able to counter, but every so often Len would get in a lucky strike. The safety padding within my costume and the metal chest protector underneath my vest and tunic absorbed most of the immediate damage, but the physical impacts would take their toll in time.

My father taught all his children how to fight and defend ourselves, and I have extended those lessons to protect those who cannot help themselves. I could hear father's voice urging me to fight honorably, but I have learned to ignore him on this matter, since there is very little honor left within the world today. I could easily defeat this louse; however, time was not on my side. Knowing their regular patrol schedule, another pair of Regulators would be along this route soon and considering how tired I was, I did not like those odds.

As Len continued to press his attack, I used my free hand to reach into one of the many storage pockets of the accessories belt along my waist and pulled out a tranquilizer dart. Normally I would shoot them via the Grapple Gun holstered on the other side of my waist, but there was no chance or point in reaching for and arming the weapon.

Instead, I allowed Len to think he was gaining the advantage over me. As he closed in for the kill, I brought up my left hand and stabbed the Regulator with the dart in the exposed area of his neck, between the lower end of Len's goggled mask and the top of his shirt collar. As the barbed tip pierced flesh, the mechanism inside released its contents into the target.

The sedative worked quickly, causing my opponent to collapse at my feet. As I saved the used dart within an empty belt pouch to be refurbished for another day and sheathed my sword, a moaning sound caught my attention. Although still face down on the sidewalk, Bill was starting to stir. I pivoted on one foot and delivered a thick boot heel to the back of his head, knocking off the tall black hat every Regulator wore in the process. Between that and hitting the cobblestones again, the man fell back into unconsciousness, totally unaware of what had transpired.

I paused long enough to make sure each Regulator's goggled mask was still in place, for despite my "villainous" reputation, I did not want any unnecessary deaths upon my hands. Then from Bill's pocket I retrieved the crumpled paper proving Mary Margaret's innocence. Not that she needed it any more, for I highly doubted the lady would ever breathe a word of this night. But now, seeking any form of senseless retribution would be a bit more difficult if my foes attempted to do so, for it was highly doubtful Bill ever bothered to see whose name was on the permit.

With that, I took my leave of the scene and cautiously made my way back to Point Hall, where the unjust now ruled the downtrodden. The site is actually two structures, but the higher one was my final destination.

Before the rise of Queen Wintersmith, the lower brick building known as The Point was New Southampton's town hall. Despite the unwanted changes in government, security within was considerably less at this late hour than that assigned the intruder perched atop it. I used my homemade passkey to let myself back in through the delivery entrance I departed earlier. Although mostly self-taught, thanks to my intense training regime, a keen mind and my high position within the realm, I easily avoided what few sentries were on duty as I made my way to the original roof via the building's old service routes.

Once upon that interim level, I crawled through the service conduits between the two structures. 'Tis not brag but simple fact that, having traversed this route so often since casting my lot in life, I could easily journey without the night vision lenses of my goggles because I long ago memorized every possible route from my handmade copies of all the classified blueprints within the royal vault.

A discreet exit via a maintenance hatch put me on the back side of the palace, in a secluded spot well away from the formal and very well guarded entryway to the royal stronghold. I was out of sight to all but the roving guard patrols. The camouflage motif of my outfit would not hide my presence completely here, for the Creeping Green was no more than mist at this height. Yet I was also too close to the edge of the abyss, so to speak. One slip and a person would fall to the street far below, so any sentry gave this spot no more than an occasional glance at best, but I would hear their approach long before I might be in any actual danger.

Noting the current weather conditions I unholstered my Grapple Gun and, from another belt pouch, armed it with the steel barbed hook that had a good length of strong, but thin rope attached. Much of my equipment was acquired from the Black Market, a place where anything available could be had for the right price. I could certainly design such tools, but had no way to create them on my own. Then again, I never said I spent *my* money there.

I would also have to acquire a new supply of gas propellant cylinders from the Royal Armory soon, but had plenty on hand to sneak in and out of Queen Wintersmith's Iron Palace. The name is derived from the iron plating that helps to maintain the interior air pressure at a constant level to keep the Creeping Green out and preserve some semblance of "normality" within. Personally, I think it was ego more than practical logistics that made Wintersmith have the five story structure erected on top of The Point. A constant reminder of who ruled New Southampton, at least for now.

Prepared, I aimed upward and sighted my target: the underside of a decorative corbel between the first and second floors that helped to support the weight of the upper levels. Squeezing the trigger gently, my projectile flew silently in the air and struck its mark true, the steel easily penetrating the iron plating and the stone beneath.

With the line firmly anchored, I reholstered the gun and pulled out my Lifter from its belt pouch. The spring that drove the built-in motor winch was wound up and ready. I tied the dangling end of the rope to the take up reel in the center of the device. Now it was just a simple matter of hanging on to the handles attached to either side of the motor works casing when I released the spring retention latch.

Activated, it began to lift me into the air while collecting the rope. I could just have easily used the line to scale up the palace side; but it was late, I was tired, and this was more fun. There was always the inherit risk of someone looking skyward at an inopportune moment, but I had composed The Rebel's outfit carefully.

A black full sleeve shirt, pants, and boots were combined with a stone-gray accessories' belt, goggled breathing mask, identity concealing hood, gloves, and short cloak. To the entire ensemble I had added irregular blotches of paint. Gray tones amongst the black items, various shades of ebony on the gray things, and all had rough splashes of color blended to match the Creeping Green. Self-produced, but quite effective camouflage in order to blend into the surroundings more naturally compared to the Regulators' red and black leather uniforms with their orange goggled breathing masks.

As the motor stopped with the last of the rope collected, I reached out with one hand and swung open what was supposed to be a secured machicolation. If the Iron Palace ever found itself under siege, the attackers could be fought in part from these secret openings along the structure.

Before closing the hatch, I paused to look out over what could be seen of miasma covered New Southampton below and the clear night sky above. But what humanity had lost and what we were struggling to hang on to, let alone regain, were not issues I was willing to face right now.

I knew well all the covert passageways, concealed chambers, and service paths within Wintersmith's castle that not even the servants traversed. That knowledge greatly aided The Rebel's cause, but for now simply assisted in stealthily reaching my private chamber unobserved.

Once secured for the night, I stored my costume and accessories within the secret compartment I built in the back of my plain, unvarnished wardrobe, and then settled down for a short nap.

Another long day of dealing with "Her Royal Highness" loomed in my future too.

***

I found it quite amusing the next day when, while within her private chambers on the top floor of the Iron Palace, Queen Anne Eliza Wintersmith started complaining once more about my alter ego.

"You lead the best trained and respected troops in all the land, second only to my personal guardians simply because their singular task is to be ever vigilant in regards to my safety. Yet you cannot apprehend a single miscreant?" she asked, angrily berating the man before her.

"The single criminal is also the hardest quarry to capture because he *is* working alone," calmly said Major Reginald Aldridge in a clip, precise response.

The leader of the Regulators of Discord was an athletic man just under six feet tall who had already seen much within his thirty-five years of life so far, hence the weathered facial features and slight touch of gray around the temples of his short, military cut hairstyle. Other than the more fanciful badge upon his chest that signified leadership, Aldridge preferred to dress exactly like the men under his command. Although wearing them was not necessary within the pressurized confines of the palace, like everyone else, he kept his goggled breathing mask in a decorative pouch attached to his belt, opposite from where his sword hung, just in case. The sky may appear clear at this altitude, but the Green's deleterious aroma was still present outside.

"How is that possible?" she demanded to know.

"Because the odds are within his favor," explained Aldridge. "A single man alone has fewer security risks compared to those of a larger ensemble. He shares his plans with no one; hence, there is no danger of betrayal. Depending upon only himself eliminates any threat of failure by others in his endeavors. Traveling alone decreases the chance of being observed and grants him more opportunities to mingle in a crowd unnoticed. Even if he worked only with the most trusted of confidantes, the fact that there were now two of them would greatly increase his hazards in the latter categories."

"I see," replied Wintersmith, thinking over what he said. "But would not the fact he works alone also increase his chance for failure? Surely the odds of his arrest lie in your favor since the Regulators seriously outnumber this lone Rebel."

"In time he will slip up and somehow make a costly mistake."

"He has already done so by daring to oppose my regime. I want that insurgent captured and thrown into the most secure cell we have for the rest of his life!" demanded the Queen, her fair face flushing an angry shade of red that almost matched the deep scar on her left cheek. "No one should flaunt my authority or interfere with the natural order of things in *my* realm."

"On those points I do agree your Majesty. However, this Rebel, as we call him - since the man has yet to come forth and deny the accusation, let alone declare his true name and intentions- has been striking at random with no logic or strategy that I can comprehend," added Aldridge. "Within this past fortnight, he attacked a Royal Tax Assessor in what passes for broad daylight within the Creeping Green and kept two of my men from making a lawful arrest."

In truth, I confiscated and destroyed the assessor's notes, for he was surveying properties that the Queen wanted to eventually claim for future projects of the Crown, with no regard for the people that would have been left homeless in the process. The "lawful arrest" was that of a butler for alleged thievery. The man donated his master's old clothing to the local church when the Earl's actual instructions were to burn them with the rubbish. While the Earl still has a vacancy to fill within his staff, his former employee is now safe and sound elsewhere.

"Then we are dealing with a madman," declared Wintersmith.

"Perhaps," conceded Aldridge. "There have been no incidents involving him for days until the wee hours of this morning, when two of my patrol men reported being accosted by this Rebel for no apparent reason other than the sheer joy of harassing them."

Besides the fact that living in The Iron Palace creates times when I am unable to slip away unobserved, I must prioritize The Rebel's public appearances because it would not do to let the Queen or anyone else realize where I am getting my information from. That would be too strong a clue as to who I really am. Despite the theoretical benefits of operating alone, if there was anyone I could truly trust with my secrets, then perhaps The Rebel would not have to let all the injustices of this realm go unchallenged. At least last night's sortie was successful. Mary Margaret and the other late working servants all reached their homes relatively safe.

"The one thing I fear is that this cad lives up to his presumed name and actually tries to incite rebellion against my regime," admitted the Queen.

That is the one thing I shall not do until a worthy successor to the throne is available. Best the devil you know…

"Cannot his arrest be expedited somehow?"

"Perhaps a bounty could be placed upon his head?" suggested Aldridge.

"No," replied Wintersmith bluntly. "Despite all my hard work on behalf of my subjects, sadly there are still dissidents amongst the people. If we only knew who this Rebel really is, we could let the judicial system deal with him without revealing all the particulars and prevent giving the public a martyr to rally around in the process."

By killing me "legally" at the first opportunity where the Crown would have no culpability.

"I can assure you that it 'tis not one of the soldiers under my command," swore Aldridge. "I would stake my life upon their loyalty."

"It already is," replied the Queen coldly. "Meanwhile, there are other matters of state to discuss. We are expecting the next shipment from our procurers—"

"I beg your pardon my lady, but should we be discussing such a delicate subject of state in front of *her*?" Aldridge asked.

Wintersmith turned and, through the open rear door of the anteroom to her private chambers, saw Jessica Gordon hard at work. Her Lady-in-Waiting was busy in the outer room of the Queen's private boudoir, straightening out and organizing the fine fashions within the Royal Armoires. The collection of tall, finely polished mahogany cabinets lined every inch of wall space not occupied by either a light fixture or the ornate entryway to Wintersmith's private bedroom.

Gordon's personal appearance, while not an embarrassment to the Crown, was far below the beauty Her Royal Highness possessed. Or at least, Anne Eliza Wintersmith would be the first to declare that fact. The Queen never allowed Gordon to wear cosmetics, and the underling always had to keep her blonde hair in a shorter, less flattering style than whatever Her Majesty wore. The Lady-in-Waiting started out her career at the Wintersmith Ironworks as our ruler's personal secretary and the Queen thought it an act of royal charity to promote Gordon to her current position upon assuming the throne, although personally I think Wintersmith just enjoys being able to order people about.

"Our Lady-in-Waiting is about as dangerous to us as a mouse is to a cat, but you are correct in your concerns for security. Come. We will discuss this, and other affairs of state, in more private environs."

But even as the Queen led Major Aldridge into her bedchamber for some amorous congress, The Rebel was already making plans.

***

Since the Crater of Noxious Adversity first appeared, the average citizen of New Southampton has lost all access to the sky. Only the taller church spires, the Iron Palace, and those aboard airships are above the Creeping Green. By what little remained visible of the day-star and the lunar light, the omnipresent fog was either brighter or dimmer as the sun tried to shine through and the lonely moon waxed and waned. Tonight, the silent orb above our war torn Earth was absent from the heavens, making the land appear even gloomier than normal. A perfect cover for those doing things they wished unobserved.

At precisely midnight, the Queen's covertly assembled motorcade left a nondescript warehouse near the Hythe Barrows port. From there, it began to traverse a roundabout route through our fair city, taking any side streets that could handle the traffic to avoid the main thoroughfares whenever possible. Once in a while I could espy a glimpse of the monorail system that helped to keep the districts united, but the procession steered clear of that too.

Our secret task force consisted of three steam powered lorries, completely flanked by Regulators riding diwheel velocipedes, either in front, behind, or alongside each vehicle. More soldiers were stationed at every intersection of the clandestine route, ensuring that the convoy passed quickly and unbothered, before returning to their regular assignments.

I was taking a serious chance this night, being a lone Rebel amongst a score of enemy combatants. But while I wore the uniform of a Regulator over my true outfit, tonight I was hopefully just another anonymous, goggled face amongst those detailed to perform this duty for the Crown. From my position on the diwheel I rode, I could see each truck was heavily loaded with wooden crates of various sizes. These containers were very valuable to Queen Wintersmith, and that made them my concern.

Soon the fleet approached our final destination: a secured building near the University of New Southampton's surviving campus. As each lorry backed into the rear loading bay of a two story Avenue Park address, I could see more Regulators of Discord everywhere. Some guarded the building's receiving area, with a couple more stationed on the fire escape above, while others were patrolling the perimeter. As I began to ride past with the rest of the velocipedes, I spied a detail of men starting to unload the cargo. The whole operation was flawlessly executed with perfect military precision. Major Aldridge would be proud.

With our escort duties concluded, the diwheels began to break formation and go their separate ways at the next intersection. I turned left and circled around, then found a discreet location in the cobblestone alley behind an off-campus housing unit for university students across the street from my objective to park and hide the velocipede in. Pocketing a stray stone, I started on my way.

Although the extra clothing and the burden of the additional materials in the bandolier I wore under the Regulator jacket would restrict my freedom of movement somewhat, especially in a fight, I kept my disguise on for now. It was best to progress as far as possible before revealing my true self. As long as no one noticed that my father's sword was vastly different, and superior, to the regulation armaments issued the soldiers, I would pass casual inspection. The uniform and vehicle were "borrowed" from a soldier who would not be found until morning. The fact that the man was currently bound and gagged after being subdued by one of my tranquilizer darts should keep him from suffering any unwarranted reprisals.

While they guarded the building's perimeter, the surrounding area was left unsecured. I covertly made my way around until facing a far corner with one lone sentry on duty. Unfortunately, he was too far away in the Green thickness to guarantee the success of a tranquilizer dart, so I would have to handle this personally.

A glance at my pocket watch revealed it was close to the next shift change. I took the stray alley stone and threw it past my target. As the man turned to check out the noise, I risked crossing the intersection, then altered my route to appear as if I was coming from the building and were the Regulator's relief.

As I saluted a "superior" officer, he asked me for the password. My response was to swiftly hit him in the throat while directly applying a tranquilizer dart to my opponent before he could raise any alarm. I am well versed in hand-to-hand combat, but without the time to prove my skills, felt no shame about executing such a cowardly attack.

The man would be unconscious for a few hours, so I dragged his body away and hid it in the dark shadows of the building across the road. Then it was just a question of waiting until the actual shift relief appeared moments later.

"Password?" I asked, disguising my voice while returning the other man's salute.

"Her Majesty," he replied.

I nodded, then took my place in line with the other Regulators going off duty. Except for what I presumed to be a fresh pair of sentries, no one else was on the loading dock. Even the lorries were gone.

The sign at the airlock entrance announced that only authorized personnel could enter this storage facility for the University of New Southampton. Not unusual in and of itself. But what were they keeping for the Queen that required so much protection?

Between the hour and the desire not to attract attention, the loading dock remained unlit at the moment, compared to "normal" operations. Since an official Regulator's goggle lenses were not as good as my own, within the effluvial environment I could barely make out the darker forms of structural beams and walls amongst the emerald mist that occupied this open area. The small lights over the airlocks to the personnel and cargo entrances were like beacons in the night, calling all wayward travelers to them.

I nonchalantly positioned myself so I would be the last one through the barrier that kept the Creeping Green out.

Out of all the dangers I faced this night, going through the airlock was when I felt the most vulnerable. If anyone was truly alert, it would be easy to trap me within the small space between the thick doors while the noxious gas was pumped out and fresh air pressurized the chamber.

Then the light over the inner door changed from red to green, an ironic color choice considering the state of New Southampton today. When the giant wheel spun and the door opened, I saluted the attendant on duty and entered the building.

Although anyone would instantly remove their goggled mask once safely inside to breathe clean fresh air, I dared not to prevent being recognized. Instead, I walked down the corridor as if knowing my way.

To my right was a sea of wooden crates of various sizes within the open, main warehouse area, which comprised most of the building. A quick pace took me to the nearest stairwell door on my left. There was no sentry or other evidence of alarms, indicating that security felt themselves safe within the building. A situation that would soon change.

I quietly ascended and, upon reaching the top step, got down on my hands and knees to cautiously peer around the corner of the staircase landing. The second floor was no more than an elongated balcony with offices along its left. The other side of the narrow aisle had a guardrail built so that anyone could look out onto the storage area. The lights were on in most of the rooms, but my interest was the warehouse floor itself.

I crawled along the floor to the balcony edge. Once there, I observed a frightening scene.

The older, balding gentleman wearing a white lab coat, accompanied by a pair of Regulators, was unexpected. I watched as the man's assistant opened each new container with a crowbar so his superior could create a handwritten inventory that would be formalized later.

But the truly terrifying sight was the contents of the shipment as each new item was pulled from the packing material within the wooden boxes so it could be accounted for.

Queen Wintersmith was amassing pre-war technology!

Long before the world started traveling down the road that took us to where we are today, Humanity has always desired to be more superior and live in a better environment than what nature originally granted us. A yearning to be smarter and stronger, while having fewer hardships and more comforts than our ancestors ever possessed. But how to do this was always a heated topic of debate.

Some, like myself, preferred the natural method: to study and train in order to grow and become a better person, while earning whatever we wanted through honest effort. Those that desired faster and greater results looked to science for the answer, but even they could not agree upon the method. While some took the latest in performance enhancing drugs despite the risky side effects, others embraced technology to improve themselves and our society.

There came a point when not only were these beings no longer truly Human, since they had transcended to what they believed was a superior plane of existence, but that no one could safely control the technology. Transhumans, rogue nanites, the anti-technology Luddites, and other factions began waging war across the globe until there was barely anything left of this once beautiful blue-green planet and the people who inhabited it. I do not know what was worse during this time, to watch my father reluctantly stay on the sidelines and guard the home front the best he could since he was no longer considered viable for battle, or to see my brothers tear our family apart when they enlisted on opposite sides of the conflict.

I sadly cannot speak for the rest of the Earth, but thankfully Doctor M. E. Fulbright appeared and started the reclamation project that is now known as New Southampton. But it was a long, uphill struggle. The nanites rendered almost everything useless before they were neutralized, and now all we have left is the modern equivalent of ancient, steam driven technology, akin to a period known as the Victorian Era over two centuries ago.

Yet now I clandestinely looked out onto a sea of relics from the past, both wondrous and dangerous. Enormous television screens and miniscule personal computers no bigger than my hand sat next to portable weapons that once emitted deadly energy discharges. There were no apparent signs that anyone had begun opening the bigger containers, but I feared what could be within them. All these items were things I had heard about either through history books or from people who actually survived those turbulent years. I never expected to see any of these devices myself.

It made a perverse sense that these things would eventually find their way here. The University of New Southampton specialized in engineering, machining, and the industrial sciences. While Queen Wintersmith may of had the foresight to amass these remnants of yesterday in hopes of keeping them out of her enemies' hands, I could easily imagine her desire that the university's scientists might be able to revive them for her own use. While some of these devices would be useful to humanity if they ever resumed working, the danger of any weapons regaining their functionality far outweighed the potential benefits.

The Queen's stockpile of ancient technology had to be destroyed! I had the means at my disposal to achieve that objective, but before I could act, the door to the corner office behind me suddenly opened!

I glanced over my shoulder and saw a Regulator emerge from the newly darkened room, as stunned to see me as I was him.

As the soldier started to move, I swung my legs in a swift kick that knocked him off his feet.

The man landed flat on his back as I pounced upon him, delivering a right fist to his jaw. While a tranquilizer dart would have been more expedient, there was no time. So before the Regulator could gain any advantage, I maneuvered behind him and applied a sleeper hold. The soldier tried valiantly not to succumb, but it was a loss cause since he was never able to even sit up under the circumstances.

While the whole incident was over in a matter of seconds, unfortunately the damage was done. “Fredrick, what's going on up there?” yelled a voice from the lower level.

Thinking quickly, I turned the unconscious man on his side and put his right hand over his chest. Then I scrambled on my hands and knees to crawl further into the office as I heard someone emerging from one of the other offices.

From behind my temporary hiding place, crouched low behind a desk, I heard a voice shout: “Fredrick's down! Possible heart attack!”

“I'll summon a medic, but start an intruder search!” ordered the man on the first floor.

A good thing the soldier really wasn't having a heart attack, considering his leader's priorities, but I had my own problems to deal with as the Regulator came further into the office. Regardless of whether or not I moved, my presence would soon be discovered. The only thing I could do was brace myself for the coming fight.

Just as the man started to come around the desk, I stuck out my left leg and intentionally tripped him. As he started to stumble I sprang up and brought my full weight to bear, forcing him down to the floor, which I made sure he met as hard as possible. With my opponent stunned, I started to apply a sleeper hold just as I heard more Regulators come up the stairs.

One of them must have been a doctor, or at least had medical training, for I heard someone announce, “His heart is healthy. He's been intentionally rendered unconscious.”

It was at that inopportune moment that the scoundrel I was fighting managed to rally one last time by kicking a nearby file cabinet before passing out, thus alerting those outside to our presence.

Letting my unconscious opponent drop to the floor, I peered around the far corner of the desk long enough to see two silhouettes back lit by the light from the storage area.

I unbuttoned my borrowed Regulator's jacket and pulled out my Grapple Gun, preloaded with a tranquilizer dart before undertaking this mission. This versatile weapon could fire a multitude of projectiles, but unfortunately only one at a time, so I would have to make this shot count.

When the office lights came on, I stood up just long enough to shoot the closest soldier. As he fell toward the floor unconscious and I ducked back behind the desk, the other Regulator did as I predicted and retreated out of the office to get more help.

I used this brief respite to my best advantage by taking off my borrowed mask and hat before rushing over to join the two soldiers on the floor near the door. With my last sparring partner still unconscious behind the desk, when the reinforcements arrived moments later, they still saw three Regulators laying on the floor in the office.

"What's going on here?" the same commanding voice that was originally downstairs demanded to know. It must have been a subordinate though, for that was not Major Aldridge speaking.

I had my back to the others, acting like I was just regaining consciousness. "It's that Rebel," I answered in my best gruff voice. "He's here in the warehouse!"

"That blighter must have fled down the back stairs. Initiate search procedures," the commander said. "Force is authorized, but the Queen wants him taken alive!"

I couldn't help smiling as the Regulators left. Although my mission had just became tougher, at least I had bought myself some time to act and my true identity was still a secret.

After re-donning the mask and hat, I opened my borrowed outer jacket long enough to remove the bandolier I wore. Of its twelve segments, most held explosive charges, but the last contained the fuses. Every volatile gray wad of destruction required a mechanical detonator, whose miniscule clockworks could delay for up to five minutes the spark necessary to set off the devastating chemical reaction.

I primed the charges by inserting a fuse into each explosive, and then donned the bandolier back over the Regulator jacket.

After intentionally leaning over the balcony, I landed on top of one of the taller crates that had not been opened yet. Fate was with me, for the container was against one of the building's six structural supports. I placed an explosive on two of the exposed metal beam's corners as high up as I could reach, setting both for the full five minutes, and then quickly worked my way down the makeshift mountain of wooden boxes to the ground.

Next I opened the large, cargo airlock door just enough for a person to slip through in preparation for a quick escape before placing my other bombs in strategic positions. With five more structural support girders to destroy, theoretically the wall with my escape route would not be directly touched, although there was enough risk of it being damaged as a consequence of the explosions. Provided I reached it in time, the airlock's thicker iron doors and walls should protect me.

I worked my way amongst the crates to the next farthest point, but could not resist pausing to help myself to a couple of bits and bobs that I secreted under my outer clothing within my rebellious outfit. While not much compared to all the wonders we lost during the war, these items would be greatly beneficial to my cause if their functionality could ever be restored.

Soon the left half of the warehouse was done, with three more support columns on the right hand side to sabotage. There was a little over two minutes left before the first explosions, so I put on the hood and goggled mask of The Rebel. This way, if I had to shed the rest of the outer disguise in a hurry, my identity would still be safe.

But just as I believed my mission would be completed without any further complications, suddenly a voice called out, “What are you doing here soldier?”

He must have come in to check on the Queen’s cache of ancient technology while the others searched for The Rebel, aka me.

Thankfully, I was still in most of my borrowed Regulator uniform with my back to the man. Its official hat kept him from noticing my mask. Thinking quickly, I turned around with military precision as if to salute a superior officer. I had every intention of physically subduing him as I completed my spin, but discovered that my opponent already had his sword drawn!

“YOU!” he shouted, recognizing my goggled mask and head covering hood. Then he lunged forward, as if prepared to kill first and ask questions later.

I managed to twist my body enough to avoid lethal contact with his sword as its sharp point sliced through the Regulator's jacket. I doubt he was expecting me to be so agile, let alone fast, for his forward momentum carried him to the point of almost stumbling over his own two feet. However he recovered quickly and turned to face me again.

I used the moment to draw father’s sword. As our blades

clashed, I studied my opponent. He was slightly taller and more muscular than me. Unlike past encounters with the Queen's men, I knew within seconds that I was facing a far more skilled opponent this time. Parries and thrusts were met and countered with ease. I used the surroundings to my best advantage, dodging and weaving whenever I could in hopes that his blade would become stuck in a crate long enough for me to put some distance between us. But he was too good a swordsman to fall for such tricks.

A slight smile crossed his unmasked face upon realizing he faced a worthy opponent, as if relishing the challenge. At least he wasn't wasting time and effort with useless banter.

Considering the quality of my past battles, I could sympathize to a point. No true sword wielder wants to become complacent and let their skills deteriorate. Yet, the chance to fully express my own talent was a bittersweet boon I did not have long to enjoy, for the clash of our weapons had brought more Regulators onto the scene.

I managed to keep him between them and me as our swords continued to speak for us, but time was running out. It was just a question of what occurred first. Would I be surrounded by every soldier on duty or...

The first two explosions were within seconds of each other. I heard the others' confused shouts as the damaged roof began to moan. A quick glance revealed that the upper half of that support and the neighboring ceiling, as well as everything within a three foot radius of them, were no longer in existence. The taller crates were now at least topless, if not completely bisected. The Creeping Green was rapidly entering the warehouse as the pure air escaped.

Regulators scrambled to don their gas masks, momentarily forgetting the conflict before them, but I will give my opponent credit. He never lost his concentration on our battle while rushing with his free hand to put his breathing apparatus on before the deadly vapors drew near. When it was in place, he began issuing orders.

"Form a detail to get the scientists safely out of here! The rest of you surround this lowly cur immediately before he can use any more explosives!" he bellowed, almost managing to disarm me in the process!

In my mind, the chances of completing this mission were dwindling rapidly. Judging by the damage, I had underestimated the bombs' strength. With two on each girder, there were only five left instead of a possible seven. The next blasts were just moments away, and it looked like I was about to be captured.

Yet my sparring partner had also given me a possible solution to my predicament too.

As the men started to approach, I swung my sword wildly in a beginner's defensive maneuver as a distraction. Everyone back-stepped to avoid being sliced, while my free hand grabbed one of the remaining munitions from the bandolier.

Realizing what I was attempting to do, my opponent seriously pressed his attack. I had to set the timer by touch and, not knowing how much time I actually had, immediately tossed it to my right as far as I could.

When I heard the explosion seconds later, at first I thought more caution would have to be exercised with the next one. But the base of the center support column on my left had lost its existence. With that and the surrounding boxes now gone, I could hear the roof in that section falling to the ground. The debris buried, if not outright destroyed, the remaining crates in that area as more of the emerald miasma that plagued the city entered.

Regulators began running, wanting to escape before they were sealed within the warehouse. As if to emphasize the need, the explosive I tossed went off, adding to the chaos around us.

Yet my opponent stood his ground and would not give up the fight. If anything, he now fought like a man possessed. We were about dead center of what remained of the storage area's right hand side, for the last explosives set before being discovered had done their job. The left half was nothing but debris as Creeping Green filled the warehouse. I saw no sign of any other Regulators.

My opponent must have surmised that the cargo airlock was now our only means of egress, for he was forcing the duel in that direction, as I contemplated how to use the remaining explosives to my best advantage. Four bombs versus three support columns. This mission may not turn out to be the success I originally envisioned, but it would at least deal Queen Wintersmith's plans a serious set-back.

Then I noticed the flames.

Something amongst the ancient armaments, perhaps old liquids or gases within the fuel cells from one of the bigger weapons, had ignited and was beginning to consume everything in its path.

Thankfully the Creeping Green itself was not flammable, but the wooden crates and packing materials added to the conflagration. While the building's brick exterior would hopefully keep the fire contained to just this warehouse, if there were any more fuel cells amongst the Queen's stockpile...

My combatant realized the seriousness of the situation seconds after I did. Given our proximity as we fought, for he had me pressed against a taller crate at the time hoping to disarm me, I could see the concern in his goggled eyes. I used his distraction to administer a good, swift kick to his groin as hard and fast as possible. As he started to double over in pain, I quickly applied the hilt of father's sword to the back of his head.

Stunned, he stumbled forward toward the cargo airlock. I made sure he became well acquainted with its iron door. Now unconsciousness, I shoved the man into the airlock. Granted, not an honorable end to the fight, but I didn't have time to worry about my conscience as something exploded within the fire!

I ran to the farthest support column on the right and set two charges on its base, both on the inward side of the metal beam. With their timers set for two minutes, I raced to the support girder closest to the airlock and repeated the procedure, but now for just one minute.

Having the four bombs basically facing each other, the force of their combined blasts hopefully would destroy much, if not all, of what lay between them. Anything remaining after the fire would only be fit for the scrapheap.

My heart felt like it was pounding within my skull instead of my chest as I raced back to the airlock and closed the thick door behind me. Sealing it, I crossed to the opposite side and began spinning the big wheel that would unlatch the outer portal and grant me freedom.

But nothing in life ever goes as smoothly as one might hope.

Just as I was starting to open the outer door, the explosions closest to my position shook the airlock and knocked me off my feet!

Regaining my footing as the sounds of the last bombs detonating was replaced by the cacophony of more building collapsing, I resumed my task, but now the door refused to open!

I shoved with all my might, and finally managed to budge it

slightly. Either some of the exterior wall had fallen the wrong way, or the loading dock itself was damaged. Whatever the explanation, debris was now blocking my escape. I kept trying to widen the exit by swinging the iron door back and forth on its hinges as a battering ram against the rubble, but in the end my efforts fell a couple of inches short of success.

In time, I knew the Regulators of Discord would dig us out. I could always use my duel opponent as a potential hostage, but that scenario would leave me seriously outnumbered without much hope for survival.

I could hear the soldiers outside scrambling to search for any potential survivors. How many unlucky Regulators might still be trapped within the warehouse was unknown, but they would definitely be looking for me. I needed to escape and make it back to the Iron Palace with my real identity unexposed so I could continue the fight another day.

That was when I remembered that, despite losing the stupid hat sometime during the fight, I still had most of my disguise on. Granted, a small detail to overlook with everything else going on, yet a crucial one in this situation.

I quickly stripped down to just my Rebel clothing. Even after unbuckling father's sword and the accessories belt from around my waist, it was still a tight fit, but I managed to squeeze through the gap to freedom.

Crawling over the fallen brick and mortar to complete my escape was not a difficult task. However, it did draw unwanted attention as a Regulator approached.

With no time for weaponry, I just simply punched the man right in the stomach, and then delivered a chop to the back of his neck that made him lose consciousness for the time I needed to clear the remains of the loading dock and run to the closest corner.

Between the intensity of the Regulator's search efforts and my camouflage, I reached my destination safely. Then I walked to the next intersection, regularly looking over my shoulder to make sure I wasn't being pursued, before going up the side street. From there, I completed a roundabout route back to where I left the diwheel behind that off-campus housing unit. I only paused long enough to observe my handiwork from the shadows of the alley before completing my escape.

Emergency service vehicles, equipment, and personnel, along with another unit of Regulators were now at the scene.

The warehouse itself was history, lost amongst the dust of its collapse and the Creeping Green. If anyone present other than the original detachment of Regulators knew what was inside and destroyed this night, they gave no outward sign that I could discern. But I knew that the soldiers would soon start spreading out in hopes of capturing a lone Rebel presumed on foot, so I walked the diwheeel another block before starting it up and taking a covert path back to the Iron Palace.

With my final destination in sight, I abandoned the vehicle and discreetly completed my journey on foot until reaching my private chamber. Although another villainous act would be accredited to the Rebel, making Queen Wintersmith even more furious with my alternate persona, at least my true identity was safe. I took great comfort in that while removing my hood and breathing mask. Running gloved fingers through my short blonde hair, I looked at the clock on my dresser and realized that Jessica Gordon only had time for a nice, long hot shower and a quick bite of breakfast before I had to wait upon "Her Majesty" once more.

***

I never set out to be a Rebel. In the beginning, I thought my position at the Wintersmith Ironworks honest employment and my eventual assignment as her personal assistant just proof of my hard work and success. But my conscience would allow me no rest upon discovering just what kind of person Anne Eliza Wintersmith really was.

I was raised properly, believing in The Golden Rule and the other tenets of what is right and wrong in life. It was then that I started refining the charade I still perform today of being totally invaluable and non-threatening, while working discreetly behind the scenes to lessen Wintersmith's cruelty toward others and at least delay her schemes whenever possible, if I cannot stop them outright.

I was as shocked as anyone else when Doctor Fulbright disappeared and Wintersmith made her play for a throne that until then, did not even exist within the democracy Fulbright was trying to sustain. It was upon her unwanted coronation when I realized it would take far more than just a good heart and the occasional covert act to thwart Wintersmith's schemes. More direct efforts would be required, and so I began developing the idea that I now personify as The Rebel.

My lot in life might not be an easy one, doing my part to keep New Southampton safe, but I must admit that there are also times when I can enjoy my unique position within the Royal hierarchy. Like when Major Aldridge, accompanied by a couple of Regulators from the warehouse, reported the night's activities to the Queen.

"HOW DARE HE?" screamed Wintersmith.

I had a moment of genuine sympathy for the Major then, for I saw him wince at the noise while a hand briefly went to his bandage wrapped head. The man had come straight from the infirmary to make his report.

"After years of research, my scientists assured me they were upon a possible solution to overcoming the nanite problem and reactivating some of the ancient technology! Do you know how much time and effort, let alone money, has gone into this project?" she bellowed, pacing back and forth in the anteroom of her chambers.

"Yes, milady," said the Major politely. "This cad has dealt the Crown a most grievous setback. It will be months before the Scroungers have acquired enough relics to begin experimentation."

The Queen stood where she was for a moment. I could see her taking a deep breath and trying to calm down as I cleared her breakfast tray. "You're right," she finally said. "We can begin anew soon enough."

"Perhaps this time the scientists could work in a secured facility right on the docks," suggested Aldridge. "Despite all our preparations, it had to be the transport convoy that drew The Rebel's attention to our actions. There is no way he could have known about the operation otherwise."

A beneficial delusion I will make sure they maintain.

"But at least that vile Rebel is now locked away in a dungeon where he can rot for the rest of his unnatural life!" said the Queen with an actual smile on her face.

"Well..." began Aldridge, before starting to recount our duel.

Not wanting to hear Wintersmith's reaction at the end of the Major's report, I walked out of the room to return the breakfast tray to the kitchen. Knowing the potential danger if they were successful, I would have to look into the scientists and their research, but that was a mission to undertake after I had a good night's sleep.

THE END, for now.

THE EYE OF THE MIND

by
Brant Fowler

This day, I awoke much the same as any other day in recent memory. Memory, ha! There I lie, staring out at the muddy sea once more, my thoughts trained on what once was and is no more, at least as far as I can reckon. It seems like I've been here, in this dreadful place, for eons now, but in reality, only a short time has passed. The sight of the green mist surrounding the city at my back is never a sight my eyes get used to. To think of the world I left to end up in this godforsaken place…

No matter. I am here now and there are things to be done. I rise up from my resting place to venture out into the grit and grime as I do every day, trying to find answers - answers that always seem to lead to more questions. I have no recollection of my coming here or what mission I was supposedly put on. All that is clear is that I don't belong here, yet, here I am.

As I contemplate my station and purpose, the bells of the city ring – such an odd thing to say considering what little I recall of my past – signifying the hour of the day. Tis eight o'clock, which means I am late. I pull on my mud-covered boots and strap on these ridiculous but very necessary goggles to protect my eyes from the green mist. "Creeping Green" is what the locals refer to it as. Sounds a bit ominous to me, but being the stranger here that I am, I give way to the colloquialism. "When in Rome" as the old saying went – a phrase I am all too sure has been long forgotten in this place. The green is somewhat familiar to me, but I do not know why.

"Top o' the mornin' to you, Mr. Littleton," says Tremley, walking around the corner to greet me as he does every morning. Littleton is my surname, or father's name as they would say here. I don't remember much of my father, so it's all I really have left of him. I constantly tell Tremley to call me Joel, my given name, but he insists on the formality for some unknown code of honor he goes by.

"Getting a bit of a late start, I see.

"The sea took my thoughts once again, friend," I reply.

"Well, best no' dwell on the sea too long lest it pull ye under wit it.'

Tremley was right, I had more important things to occupy my time. Tremley was a good man who showed me great kindness from the day I set foot in this town of New Southampton. He was the first living soul I laid eyes on after crawling out of that tube. He was not a man of great wealth or importance, but one of great kindness. I wandered the streets, aimless, confused, and nearly naked but for a blanket I snatched from an absent vagrant's stash. When Tremley came into view that night those many months ago, I was preparing myself for the worse. The man was not of great stature, but average height and build. His clothes suggested modest means. His hair, with patches of gray appearing, betrayed his age. Even still, in the shadows, in my precarious state, I feared for my safety. But instead his hand extended to meet mine and his mouth widened in a gentle grin. He brought me in to his humble abode and offered me nourishment. Ever since, we have been friends of a sort, looking out for one another. This morning was no different. Good old Tremley was looking out for me. In my *profession*, if that is what you can call it, it does not pay to be late. Nor does it pay to dwell on dreams of another life I shan't have again.

"Right you are," I say. "Best be off."

"Good luck!" Tremley said. Then, a little bit lower, but still audible, he said "You'll need it."

You'll need it. Every morning, Tremley sends me off with those words muttered under his breath. And every morning truer words are never spoken. Given my lack of proper papers, it is nearly impossible for me to find a legitimate means of supporting myself. So I have had to rely on… other means to get by - means that aren't always the safest. Fortunately, I have my own ways of protecting myself from such dangers. Still, it pays not to be overconfident when dealing with the manner of men I meet on a daily basis.

As I walk through the underbelly of the great city, I can't help but marvel at the structures that are so different from my true home. At times, it's like looking at a history book from my youth or a period piece film. I miss those. Sure, some of the buildings are in various states of disarray, especially in this seedy part of town. But others have been restored to what some consider one of the most influential periods of our history. A time of supposed peace and prosperity, though from what I recall, it too had areas such as this, where beggars and thieves ran rampant. It was the only way to survive for those of lesser means. Seems to me as much as the world changes, the more it remains the same. Even in these dark and perilous times, the societal hierarchy seems to be intact. Pity, that.

"You're late," a voice says, calling out to me from the shadows of the alleyway, snapping me back to the present. It's Gunderson, the man I've come to meet as I do every day. He's tall and lanky, save for his swollen belly. He reeks of cheap ale and fish. His long brimmed hat, tattered gray shirt and suspenders put me in mind of an old-time cowboy fallen on hard times. His overgrown and limping black mustache finishes the image and makes for a distinction one doesn't soon forget. I've tried to convince him that such a garish display would make him easier to pick out in a crowd, but he insists it gives him character.

"I apologize for my tardiness, Mr. Gunderson—"

"Ain't no mister, Littleton. And don't go giving me yer excuses, just get inside. Now."

I nod and lead the way inside the small back room we have taken up for our daily meetings. The room is not quite as small as an oversized closet, but not much larger either. There is room only for a table, a few chairs, a safe and a smaller table over to the side. One might think that a room such as this, off in some alley might not be the most secure place to house a safe, but they would be wrong. There is always someone here, and armed. Only Gunderson's most trusted men remain with the safe, watching guard, which is precisely why I must make the trek here every day. Not because I am trusted but because I am not. Otherwise, I might be set for this task.

Waiting inside the room is today's guardsman, a man simply known as Branch. It is unclear whether that is this mountain of a man's real name or a nickname given to him. Standing well over six feet in height, with arms chiseled from stone, some say he is called Branch because of his tree-like appearance. Others say it's because getting hit by him is like taking a solid tree branch to the face. Either way, he is not a man to cross. Hardly ever speaking a word, Branch glares at me as I enter the room. Tis hard to say whether this is because he doesn't like me or trust me or if this is just his way. After all, he looks through everyone all the same, in equal measure, even Gunderson.

"If you weren't so useful I'd have Branch 'ere take ye out in the alley for making me wait, Littleton."

"I guess it's fortunate for me that I am useful then."

Gunderson pauses, looking at me intently before continuing on.

"Well, we'll see just how useful ye are today, eh? There's a new shipment comin' in. I need ye to find out the carriage's route and report back t'me. Can ye handle that?

"You know that I can and I shall. Provided the payment is worthy of my… talents, of course."

"Of course."

I don't like the way Gunderson smirks as he says this. Today feels different all of a sudden, and I'm not sure why. I use my talents restrictively for the weight they carry. Something tells me, though, the risk might be warranted this time.

I stare directly at Gunderson, focusing, concentrating. I try to get a read on him, see what he is thinking. I don't know how or why I have these abilities, or to what end. All I know is that when I want to, I can see inside a man's thoughts and they betray his intent to me. The course is taxing, though, and takes its toll on me. As I peer into Gunderson's mind, my suspicions are confirmed. He means to betray me, then kill me. He has found another means of gaining his wealth, and his distrust of me has grown, but why?

"What're ye lookin' at? Did ye not unnerstan?"

I don't have a chance to dig deeper. As I continue to stare, Gunderson's hand reaches beneath the table to the revolver strapped there. A rare item in these times, but one he came about all the same. My staring has made him nervous. Behind me,

Branch has leaned forward, ready to pounce if so instructed. I am forced to break contact for self preservation.

"My apologies Mr... Gunderson. I felt a bit light-headed and was trying to steady myself."

Gunderson's grip on the revolver loosens and his body relaxes. Branch is also at ease, leaning back and crossing his arms about his chest.

"Yer a strange one, Littleton. But no mind. Off with ye, find my carriage, then meet me back here in two hours. Can ye handle that, or might ye fall over from all the excitement?" Gunderson begins to laugh at my expense, but I don't mind given the alternative.

"I shall be fine. Two hours it is, I shall see you then."

I know from what little I was able to glean from Gunderson that he has no intention of meeting me here in two hours, nor does he expect me to be able to return at all. Gunderson's other goons are following me, I can hear them. Not their footsteps, but their thoughts alert me to their presence. They are lurking about in the shadows as I traverse the maze-like alleyways of the inner city Ruins, a name some of the lesser folk have come accustomed to calling the area. I try to read their thoughts as to throw them off my trail, but the headaches have already begun. The price I pay for using the ability, I'm afraid. I must elude these men and soon.

Since I can't use my ability to gain a foothold, I rely on my other skills. I have been living here and performing these tasks long enough to know my way around quite well. I know the shortcuts and secret passageways of this city as well as anyone. In my trade, I have to, or I am a dead man, or worse. I lead Gunderson's men to the busiest section of the Ruins, where beggars and traders galore scatter throughout the streets, causing a sea of under the table commerce and back alley dealings. I read their thoughts long enough to discern they have lost sight of me for the moment as I duck behind a merchant selling women's cloaks and other accoutrement. I take the opportunity to snatch one, draping it about me, as I dart down the street to my left, effectively losing the pair of them. After traveling down the street a piece, I mentally scan the area to make sure I'm alone. Satisfied that I am, I find a dark corner and prepare for the coming onslaught in my head.

What little light there is begins to fade as my eyes close from the intense strain. The darkness, though, is soon replaced by searing light in my mind's eye as the visions, I call them, begin to take form. I try to stifle my screams as not to alert anyone to my presence, but it proves difficult. I only used my ability a short time, so the pain is more manageable, but still not a small thing. I see glimpses of a time passed – one of great technology. Motorized vehicles buzzing about, artificial lighting filling rooms. Then I see images of a great war – a war I was present for, but not. Much death and tragedy and then the world goes dark.

As I begin to gain my senses once more, I hear voices. At first, I think them in my head still. But as my eyes open as slits, I can make out blurred visages of men standing over me. In fear, I think these are Gunderson's men, meant to do me in. My arms thrash about, trying to free myself of their grasp, but they just hold on more intently. I try to get to my feet to properly defend myself, but one of them pushes me back down against the wall. I am panicking, feeling that all this has been for naught. All these long months of getting close to the underground, trading for information has led me to nothing but death in an abandoned alley where I'm likely to never be found.

I have all but given up hope when something deep down inside of me rushes over me, consuming me with energy and will to live. My arms are restrained, I am being held down and yet I find myself determined to struggle free. With all my might, I see myself tossing these men aside and fleeing for my life, and so that's what I do. First, the man to my left goes flying backwards falling over some trash bins. After him, the one on my right is knocked straight down to the grown, smacking his head on the hard stone. And finally the man in front of me, the one who pushed me back down, goes hurtling backwards, crashing hard into the wall opposite me. As I come fully to my senses I realize I haven't moved an inch.

As I find my footing, I look about to ensure these men are all down and won't be able to follow me. But I do not find Gunderson's goons lying before me. Instead, these are common traders, probably just trying to help me. They undoubtedly heard my screams and rushed to my aid. I repaid them with violence, and in one case, death. The man that held me down, he hit the wall so hard it seems to have taken the life from him. He sits as I did, propped against the wall, wide and horrified eyes staring back at me, unblinking.

"How…" I say to myself, but audibly as well, so great is my disbelief. *This has never happened before*, I think to myself. My ability is in the reading of others' thoughts – telepathic we would call it in my time. This is something different altogether.

"What is happening to me?"

Having had enough excitement for one day, I head back to Tremley's for some much needed rest. I have been careful not to reveal my living quarters to those whom I deal with, but still I worry they will find me. I must take the risk, though. It's the only place I am somewhat safe, and these events have taken a lot out of me. Tremley is there waiting for me, almost as if he was expecting me.

"I see you're back early, eh, Mr. Littleton?"

"Rough day."

"I'd say so from the looks 'o ye. Come on in and have a lie down. You'll feel better after a nice long nap, ye will."

"Thanks, Tremley, you're too kind to me."

"Someone 'as to be, now don' they?" Tremley then flashes me that same gentle grin he first greeted me with those many months ago. I then retire to my bed and let sleep take me over.

In my dreams, my mind reaches out across the city. Gunderson is meeting up with the goons he sent after me, and he does not look pleased.

"What do ye mean ye lost 'im? How 'ard could it be to keep up wit that one?" said Gunderson.

"Please, sir, he just vanished into the crowd," begged one of the goons.

"Yeah, like magic, he did. One minute he was there, then POOF, he was gone," said the other goon.

"Magic, eh? Branch here knows a thing or two about magic. For his next trick he's gonna make the lot of you disappear, would ye like that?" Branch snatches the two goons up by their collars, one in each hand.

"Wait. WAIT! You'll want to be hearing this."

"Go on, then," Gunderson said as he motions for Branch to let the man go. The man composes himself then continues.

"We heard reports of a man passed out in an alley not far from where we lost Littleton. They says he woke up in a fit and killed those that helped him on the spot without lifting a finger."

Gunderson considered this for a moment, then motioned for Branch to continue with his magic trick.

"No, it's true, it is!" cried the other man. "The way I heard it he, Littleton, was trying to get up and them's that helped him was trying to steady him. He just lashed out and theys went flyin' through the air."

"Hmm," said Gunderson, "maybe there's more to our Mr. Littleton than we knew. We may have use for him yet."

"So we did good, yeah, boss?"

"Yeah, we don't need to be seeing no magic tricks today me thinks."

"Oh, but Branch has been practicing and is eager to show off his skills, boys. Ye wouldn't want to disappoint him, now would ye?" Gunderson let out a hearty laugh as Branch dragged the goons away kicking and screaming.

Several hours later, I awoke once more in that same shack facing the sea, but my thoughts were not upon it this time. Instead, covered in a cold sweat, I thought intently on the scene that played out in my dreams. Was it real? Could it be? I can read minds, but I have never read them in my sleep to my knowledge. Nor have I reached out so far from my location and viewed events I wasn't present for. Then I consider the visions I have when my headaches come on. Is this the same?

Regardless, I can't take the chance. If Gunderson thinks he has use for me, he will stop at nothing to find me. And if he finds me, he'll find…

"TREMLEY!"

I rush out of my room, running to find my friend that took me into his home and saved me from God knows what fate. I am relieved to find him sitting by the fire with dinner in the kettle, awaiting me to join him before dining.

"What are you on about, Mr. Littleton? Screaming out my name and all."

"I-I'm sorry, friend, I was plagued by a bad dream."

"Ye seem to be havin' lots of those lately, eh?"

"What do you mean?"

"For two weeks straight now you've been thrashing about in your sleep, muttering this or that. Talk of things I don' unnerstan fully."

"I-I did not know."

"You, not knowing something, now that's something, that is. Wat wit your gift and all." Tremley winks at me as he says this and it unnerves me. I've never told Tremley about my ability. How does he know?

"I do not know what you refer to, friend…"

"Oh, come now, Mr. Littleton. Ye don't go livin' with someone for as long as we have and not get to know them. Ye know things at times no man could know. Why, the first time I laid eyes on ye, ye called me by name before I even introduced meself."

He's right! I had forgotten that, but I had. As I stumbled through the dark and saw his hand extend, I said the word "Tremley" to him. I remember now – it's always so hard to remember. He looked at me surprised yet somehow knowing and then flashed that smile I would come to associate with the man. How could I have forgotten that? And what more does Tremley know? Can I confide in him?

"Tremley…" I start, but before I can finish my thought, we are interrupted by an all too familiar voice.

"There ye be," called out Gunderson as he came into view by the fire's light, flanked by Branch and three other men I had never seen before.

"Mr. Littleton and I were about to sup, would ye care to join us?"

"Mister? Well, ain't that rich. Littleton here ain't no gentleman. And from the looks o' ye, ye ain't neither."

"I see you have gotten yourself some new help, Gunderson."

"Good help is hard to find. Branch here had to… share some of his talents with the old guard."

So it's true! My dream, it did happen. Gunderson had Branch kill those two goons that followed me. And worse, they know what I can do.

"Cut to the chase then, why are you here? What do you want with me?"

"Isn't it obvious? You and I have unfinished business, Littleton. Ye missed our meeting and I don't have me carriage. So as I see it, ye owes me money. And pay you will."

"And if I refuse?"

"Then Branch might just have to share some of his talents with your friend here."

With a nod, Branch yanked Tremley from his seat, holding him off the ground.

"ALRIGHT! Alright, just please, put him down and leave him out of this. He has nothing to do with our… arrangement."

"Oh, but he does. He's harboring ye, which puts him in direct opposition with me. If ye don't come through, he ain't gonna be makin' no more suppers for you or anyone. In fact, I think ol' Branch will stay here and keep an eye on him while you and I discuss a new arrangement, Littleton."

Wary though I was, I had no choice. I knew not how I had unleashed my newfound ability in the alley, so I had no immediate means of defending myself against five men, let alone poor Tremley. I had no choice but to go with Gunderson and do his bidding. Not for my sake, but for Tremley's. He had shown me so much kindness and generosity these past months. I could not in good conscience repay that with abandonment and disregard for his life. But, even though I had no control over this ability, I would use their knowledge of it to my advantage.

"Fine, then, let's be on our way. But if one hair on Tremley's head is harmed, what I did to those men in the alley will seem like child's play."

"Well, well, so it *was* you. That might just come in handy. But point taken. No harm will come to your friend so long as ye don't betray me again."

That came off a bit more brash than I had anticipated, but it did achieve the effect I was hoping for all the same. Of course, I know all too well how little Gunderson's word means, especially after today. I had to play this smart so as not to endanger Tremley's life or my own.

We arrived at a place uptown that I had never been. It was of a higher standard than the less desirable alleys of the Ruins, but not quite up to the standards of the Queen's court and that area of town. This place was somewhere in the middle. In years past, this place might be akin to the suburbs, the dwellings of the middle class. I wondered why we met here instead of the usual place, but knew better than to ask questions. Besides, if I really wanted to know, I could simply read Gunderson's thoughts to find out. That information didn't seem important enough to warrant the risk at this time. As I was contemplating this, a man approached. Then I understood why we were meeting here. He was a man of a higher station, dressed in fine threads and possessing a stature indicative of three square meals a day and then some. He was in his late 30s to early 40s by the looks of him, his hair already starting to run from his forehead. Meeting here, twixt the Ruins and the Queen's court, was akin to slumming it for this man. He wouldn't dare come anywhere near the Ruins, but here, he could make do. But why was a man of his import meeting with Gunderson of all people? Of course, that answer couldn't be any more obvious.

"Gunderson," said the man.

"Duke," replied Gunderson.

"Shush! Do not use my title!"

Duke? This isn't any average gentleman, he's a noble!

"My apologies, *sir,*" Gunderson said with obvious contempt. He wasn't thrilled to be having this meeting. And frankly, meeting with a noble makes me every bit as nervous.

"Is this him?" the Duke asked.

"Yessir, that's him. He can get the job done for ye, no problem."

"Excuse me, but what job exactly?"

"Haven't you told him anything?"

"We were just about to get to that when you walked up, *sir*. But I figured he probably already knew anyhow."

Gunderson may not have been an educated man but he wasn't an idiot either. He discerned my ability after a while. Now I wish I had read his thoughts on the way here. I have stepped into this blindly and now find myself in leagues with a supposed royal! Even though Gunderson suspected what my ability was, I had never outright told him. So I continue the charade. I don't want to trouble myself and take the risk if I don't have to.

"How would I know if you have not informed me, Gunderson?"

Gunderson did not like this approach as it made him look stupid. But without Branch here, and fearing my newfound ability, he had no recourse but to swallow it and speak the plan aloud.

"That would be my oversight then, Littleton." He glowered at me with such hatred I had no need to read his thoughts to know what he was thinking at that moment.

"The Du—good sir here has provided us with a way to... expand our business in exchange for a few small favors. Favors ye will perform without hesitation. Do we understand each other?

"Perfectly. So, what are these favors I am to perform?"

"Thanks to Gunderson's slip of the tongue, you know of my importance in this city. Let us just say that I wish to have even greater importance and require your assistance to bring that to pass."

"Your contemporaries have secrets you wish to expose in order to further your own political and societal station."

"…Gunderson, you surprise me, affiliating with such intelligent parties. Yes, yes that's it exactly. You do not disappoint."

"I rarely do."

Gunderson is livid at being showed up yet again. Unintentionally, I can hear his thoughts of contempt for me and the many ways he wishes to dispose of me. Ever since the alley and those men I incapacitated, my abilities have been freer and even less controlled. As I ponder this development, though, I hear something far more disconcerting.

This may be the one she is looking for after all. This fool, Gunderson has brought his pride and joy right to me and handed him over. I may not even need his abilities to gain the Queen's favor.

The Duke looks my way and sees that I am staring at him and immediately breaks his train of thought, muttering random strings of words in his mind trying to block my reading them. *Teddy bears, eggs, mimes dancing on elephants.* It's quite amusing watching him scramble to disguise his thoughts. I'd almost smile if I hadn't just heard his plans for me. I am to be at the mercy of the Queen, and somehow she knows about my abilities!

"Ahem, well, yes, hmm… we should get on with it, then. Gunderson, have Mr. Littleton brought to the arranged place tomorrow morning at six o'clock sharp. You will receive the other half of your payment then." The Duke says as he tosses down a sack of currency before walking away.

"He'll be there with bells on," Gunderson says as he picks up the sack, looking back at me with a wicked smile, not realizing he's been duped out of a greater prize. He could have used me to gain far greater wealth and stature within the city. That is, of course, if I allowed it. Gunderson I could handle, even manipulate if it came to it. This Duke, on the other hand, is cause for concern.

"And what is my payment for this new arrangement, Gunderson?"

"Yer life and that of yer friend's ain't enough? Getting greedy, are ye, Littleton?"

"Considering what you now know I can do, what makes you think I'll show up to assist the Duke, let alone let you and your crew live?" It's a risky move, taunting him like this, but it is all I have.

"Fine, fine, don't get your britches in a twist. Ye want more information about wat yer doin' here. I can give that to ya. Though it makes no sense to me."

It did not make much sense to me either, what information I had gathered from my previous dealings with Gunderson and other unsavory figures in the Ruins. When I first was found by Tremley, I didn't remember much at all of my life before climbing out of the tube. Little by little, the flashes would come, haunting me of times past, but never giving me a full picture. I knew not where, or when, I came from, but I knew the world had changed. This was not the world I last saw, and all that consumed me was finding answers to fill in the gaps. Tremley reluctantly pointed me towards information traders in hopes what little I could find would quell my thirst for knowledge of my past. These individuals somehow came upon details of the world gone by and would sell them in return for goods. With my ability, I could walk through an alley, listening in on people's hidden conversations and determine the best and easiest scores. This gained me favor and I rose amongst the ranks, getting what information I could. Gunderson seemed to be the greatest source of that information. Now I wonder if he wasn't getting it straight from the Queen's court.

All I had been able to discern to date was that the world once thrived with technology before a great war tore the world down. And that during that time there were people with enhancements that could do strange things. Those people were the cause of the war. They were called Transhumans. The rest of the information I gathered was only about how New Southampton came to be and about the Creeping Green. I was no closer to understanding who I was or where I came from than when I began this quest, not really. But learning this information triggered the memory flashes and eventually, most recently, the dreams. I was getting closer.

"What information can you give me that I don't already know?"

"How 'bout where you came from? Would that do?"

Before I could answer, I heard thoughts – lots of thoughts – surrounding us. Seemingly out of nowhere, we found ourselves surrounded by a small army of men, the Queen's Regulators of Discord. This is why the Duke was masking his thoughts. He didn't want to give away his double cross. He had no intention on dealings with me or Gunderson. He meant only to capture me.

"By order of the Queen, you are under arrest!" shouted a middle-aged man just under six feet tall with an athletic build. He seemed to be the leader of the men. He and the Regulators were adorned in red and black leather with orange goggled breathmasks to protect them from the Creeping Green. Some were on foot while others sat upon their single-wheeled velocipedes.

"You heard the Major!" shouted one of the Regulators, whom I assume was his second in command. "Surrender and no harm will come to you."

"Yet…" snickered another of the guard under his breath, which resulted in several others joining him in the laugh.

"Silence!" yelled the Major, reprimanding his men for their lack of decorum. "Let us take these men in and be done with it. Enough of this tomfoolery!"

The Major seemed to be a serious man, duty bound, and his thoughts confirmed it. This bade well for me as he would not stand for the Regulators to take their liberties with us. That had no bearing, of course, on my fate once I was delivered to the Queen, but for now I remained safe. Well, as safe as one could hope to be in custody under monarchy rule.

We were hauled away in shackles to be brought before the council on the morrow. I was so close to the answers I sought. For this to happen now… if only I could call out my ability. As I contemplated this course of action, a swift knock on the head by the butt of a nightstick sent me to my dreams once more. It appears I was wrong about the Major's intent to keep us safe. Maybe he was trained to protect himself from my ability and mislead me to a false sense of security, however fleeting. No matter, I would end up at the same place regardless, at the Queen's mercy.

"I seek audience with the Queen," said the Duke I had met earlier that night.

"State your business," replied the guard at the Iron Palace, the massive structure in the center of the city that hosted the self-imposed Queen and her royal court.

"I have found the one she seeks."

"Wait here."

After a few minutes, the guard returned, notifying the Duke that the Queen would see him now. The Duke stood before her majesty, grinning from ear to ear. The Queen, Anne Wintersmith, is stunningly beautiful, with long dark hair and piercing green eyes. If not for a scar on her cheek and an evil countenance about her, she would be flawless. She sat in her perch, eying the Duke with disdain, barely listening.

"You say you found the one I seek. And which one is that, pray tell?"

"The one… with abilities, my Queen," said the Duke in hushed tones, taking care to avert his eyes from her.

The Queen perked up at this news, now curious and paying full attention to the Duke.

"Do go on. How do you know this is the one?"

"I… have dealings with those that have experienced his gifts firsthand."

"And you have brought him to me?"

"He is en route now, my Queen. We shall have audience with you on the morrow if you so desire."

"You will bring him in as soon as he arrives, Duke Farthington. Is that clear?"

"Y-yes, your majesty. Straight away."

"Then be off and see to it!"

"Begging your pardon, my Queen, but what of my r-reward?"

"Go see that he is brought to me immediately or a reward will be the least of your concerns. And don't inquire of me again about your gain in this matter!"

I am woken abruptly to have audience with the Queen of New Southampton, I'm told, confirming my dream yet again. I now know for certain she is seeking me, but for what cause? How does she know of me and what I can do, things that are even a mystery to me? I have no time or chance to think on this further as I am cleaned up and sent to see the Queen as soon as I arrive at the Iron Palace. It is the first time I've seen it up close, save in my dreams. It is as glorious and terrifying as descriptions of it portray it to be. I am overwhelmed by its intensity, yet somehow comforted by its security.

Inside, I am shuffled off straight away to have audience with the Queen, as she commanded. I am told not to look her in the eye and to bow before her. Hearing the guards' thoughts, I choose to follow this advice lest my life be taken from me for the insult.

Here I stand before the Queen, ready to hear my fate. I do as I was told. I bow and avert my eyes, staring at the ground. All the while, I try to train my senses on the Queen's thoughts, but to no avail. For some reason, my abilities are failing me at this crucial moment.

"Are you trying to read my mind, Mr. Littleton?" the Queen asks me.

"My Queen?" I inquire, trying once again to deny my abilities to those interested in them.

"No need to be coy with me, Mr. Littleton. I am fully aware of what you can do and I assure you I mean you no harm."

"You disarm me, my Queen. I have no defense, nor response."

"That is *my* gift, Mr. Littleton. Though not as extraordinary as yours, it has served me well." She gives a slight grin, which I find most alarming.

"Now, Mr. Littleton, I want you to know that I have been looking for you for a long time. I wish you to be in my service from here on out. Are these terms agreeable to you?"

"Begging your pardon, my Queen, but those don't seem like terms at all as there is nothing to gain on my end. Rather, it is a mandate. And as such, what does my reply matter?"

"Ah, a clever one you are, Mr. Littleton. Very well, you have me all figured out and without even reading my mind. You'll find that a difficult task, by the by. As I said, I know of your abilities and have spared no expense finding ways to defend myself from it."

As I suspected, the Queen has prepared for my coming and likely prepared her most trusted charges as well. This is why the Major was able to mislead me earlier.

"Then you have me at a disadvantage, my Queen. What is it

that you require of me?"

"To the point, I like that. You are no doubt aware of the various rebel groups that plague this city, wishing to depose my reign?"

"I am."

"Then is your mission not clear?"

"You wish me to use my abilities to ferret them out for you so you can rid the city of them once and for all."

"And here I thought you couldn't read my mind. Maybe I didn't pay enough for these preventive measures."

"I assure you, my Queen, no mind-reading was necessary to discern your wishes for me. I have come accustomed to people wanting to use my gifts to… illuminate things for them."

"Illuminate. An interesting choice of word considering this other ability of yours I'm told. A light flashes and three men die at your hand without ever so much as raising a finger? No, Mr. Littleton, you misunderstand me. I don't wish you only to 'illuminate' threats against the crown. I wish you to 'eliminate' them. Is this something you can do for me?"

This revelation finds me at a loss. I am no killer, at least not intentionally. But if I refuse, not only will I die but Tremley as well, if he still lives. I cannot risk his life nor mine. The thought of serving the Queen in this manner is revolting. I know not much about the Queen, but what I have learned suggests her to be the vilest of individuals, ruling from a place of power, not right. And having met her my opinion in that direction is only greater. But if I were to refuse then I would have no hope and my entire quest, my entire life, would mean nothing.

"Not that I am left with much choice in the matter, your majesty, but yes, you have my word. I will do this thing for you. I do have one request, however, if it pleases the Queen."

"Speak it."

"I have a friend at the sea, goes by the name of Tremley. I ask only for his safety. He has shown me a great kindness since I came to this place and I wish to repay it in kind if I may."

"Has this Tremley ever committed any act against the crown, Mr. Littleton?"

"To my knowledge he has not. He is a simple man that lives by the sea. He is of harm to no one."

"Then you have my word he will be protected. Let it not be said that your Queen is not just."

"Thank you, my Queen. I am indebted to your grace."

"Indeed you are, Mr. Littleton. Indeed you are. Now off with you."

I am led away to my chambers for the night, feeling that I have sold my soul to the devil. My only comfort is that I have saved Tremley, my only friend, from a fate far worse. I have done things I'm not proud of since coming to New Southampton, since crawling out of that tube. I can attempt to justify those actions by claiming the quest for knowledge of my past as motivation. But it is an empty gesture. The path I have chosen has brought me here, in the service of the hated and feared Queen Anne Wintersmith.

As sleep takes hold of me once more, I dream of the Queen. Her thoughts are shielded from me when I am in her presence, but apparently not while I am asleep. Perhaps her defenses are down. I know not. But I watch and I listen unintentionally as I have been for the past few days whenever sleep takes me.

"So, you found him after all this time?" a man I have not laid eyes on before inquires of the queen. His features are obscured from me, save for a long, black cloak lightly disguising a slim and fit figure. He's about my height and very refined. He speaks to the Queen with a familiarity rather than that of a subject or even another noble.

"I did. What of it?"

"If he is whom we have sought then plans are in motion and the tide will turn. There will be no opposition that can thwart us. Not even if Fullbright himself returned."

"Speak not of that name in my presence!"

"My dear, I am not one of your underlings you can order about. Do not forget to whom you speak."

"I know well of whom I speak to. You should not forget to whom you speak, either."

After an intense moment of equal stares, the two share a hearty, knowing laugh.

"My, you have not changed at all, dear sister."

"Nor you, dear brother. Now, about Mr. Littleton. What do you plan to do with him after we have eliminated the rebel factions?"

“Once we have no use for him any longer, we shall dispose of him. We can’t have one of his… reputation here, in the present. There’s a reason they were all done away with in the first place. His very existence could bring this entire kingdom crumbling down around us.”

“Very true. I’ve already sent for this Tremley he spoke of. He will be brought to the dungeons. After Mr. Littleton has fulfilled his use, we shall kill them both.”

“And what of the Duke and those he associates with?”

“They are being dealt with as we speak. No one can know about Mr. Littleton or his abilities.”

I sit up straight in my bedroll, cold sweats taking me once more. The Queen’s plan is clear to me now, yet I know not what to do. I could find a way out of here, but then what of Tremley? Tremley, poor Tremley. I have unwittingly betrayed him by the mere mention of his name. It is because of me that he has been brought to this place. It is because of me that his kindness will be repaid with death.

Perhaps I could use my abilities to rescue us both. The Queen did say that she was going to lengths to eliminate those who know about me and my abilities. Surely the Major will not be dismissed in that nature, but anyone else who knows. This could work. But this Queen knows more about me and where I come from than I can fathom.

No, I can’t leave. I must stay close and learn all that I can. Learn to control these dreams if that is possible. Learn to use this other ability of mine and find a way to help the rebel forces.

Over the next several weeks, I patrol the Ruins, searching the minds of those around me, trying to piece together clues to where the resistance camps are located. I get close several times, but I quickly learn the rebels never stay in one place too long. They are smart in this way, moving from one base of operations to another. It makes it harder to track them. But eventually someone will either slip up or I will happen upon a rebel whose thoughts betray their location. After all, only the Queen and her most trusted council know the truth of my abilities.

Today, I am to patrol the south end of the Ruins, an area I have not yet covered. Going on foot, trying to decipher and read the minds of so many people, it takes a toll, so it is a very time consuming venture. But a thought I picked up earlier in the week pointed me in this direction. I'm told I will be accompanied by someone new today, someone who is supposed to be able to help me.

"Well, well, well, look where we find ourselves now, Littleton."

It can't be… Gunderson! I was sure he was disposed of for knowing my secret. But here he stands before me, wicked grin and all. There's not even a scratch on him. I try to read his thoughts to gain a measure of where he has been and what he's up to but something's wrong. I can't break in.

"Ah-ah-ah, Littleton. Ye won' be invadin' me thoughts anymore. The Queenie…" Gunderson catches eyes with the disapproving Regulators lingering about and changes his tone quickly. "Er… her majesty took care o' that fer me. Ye won' be havin' no advantages o'er ol' Gunderson no more."

That slimy countenance and devilish smirk across his face bring me to anger, but I mustn't let him get to me. I discern that this entire time, the Queen and her charges have been training Gunderson to protect himself against my ability, that's why I haven't seen him. Which tells me two things. One, it's a lengthy process, and two, the Queen is unhappy with the results I've given. Gunderson confirms my suspicions.

"See, Littleton, the Queen don' feel like ye've been puttin' yer best foot forward, so as to speak. I'm here to make sure ye ain't playin' her for a fool."

The mere mention, nay thought, of the Queen taken for a fool did not sit well with the Regulators as they rushed to Gunderson's side to set him straight.

"You will watch your tongue where it concerns the Queen, slum-slime. Any further disrespect shown the throne will not end well for you."

"Rest easy, big fella, I didn't mean nothin' by it. Besides, the Queen needs me. Ye best be rememberin' that, ye ought."

SMACK!

Gunderson goes down in a heap on the ground, holding his jaw after a vicious backhand by the Regulator.

"You are a tool at best, Gunderson. A tool that can and will be replaced. You best remember that!"

Gunderson warily eyes the Regulator as he dusts off his hat and replaces it upon his head. He then turns slightly, looking at me out of the corner of his eye to gauge my reaction. I stand solemn, not wishing to give Gunderson any further fuel to fire his contempt for me. After all, though he may just be the Queen's tool, he is still in her charge and thus in a position to make life very difficult for me and, more importantly, for Tremley. Though my kind friend's life is already in danger, I wish not to cause him pain in the meantime.

I then extend my hand to the still knelt Gunderson, offering to help him to his feet. He pushes my hand away hastily and clamors up on his own, not willing to accept the assistance. As much is to be expected, though. I never intended him to take my help. Gunderson may be a vile and despicable man, but he is yet a proud one.

"Let's git on with it, then, Littleton. We ain't got all day." Gunderson spat.

We break away from the Regulators and proceed into the south end of the Ruins, down some narrow alleyways where all kinds of criminal activity takes place. Everything from the simplest of offenses like street gambling to the more serious crimes of fencing and prostitution. Anything these people can do to survive they do here.

Gunderson moves in close, attempting to intimidate me to no avail.

"Ye got anything yet?" he whispers.

"We've only just arrived," I reply. "I've been at this for weeks. I'm not going to stumble onto something in the first five minutes."

"Don' be playin' with me, Littleton!" he says, slightly raising his voice. "Who's to say you ain't been holdin' out? That's why I'm here in the first place, don' you ferget!"

"I am cautious," I tell Gunderson, "but I am no fool. I know mine and my friend's lives hang—"

Just as I was retorting, I catch a flash. A simple phrase: "The red five." It comes from a smallish man in a brown tattered coat and gray, wide brim hat wandering to and fro, from door to door, looking intently upon each one before moving on to the next. He seems fearful… no, anxious. He wants to find his destination speedily. In between doors and repeated thoughts of the phrase, his eyes dart about as to check to see if he is being followed or watched.

I snap back to myself as I realize I had practically gone into a trance listening to the man's thoughts. And Gunderson noticed as well. His breath is close upon me once more.

"What is it? You heard somethin', didn' ye? What was it?"

I hesitate before answering, which angers Gunderson. He grabs me by the shirt and shakes me, beading down on me, his eyes filled with anger mixed with… fear? Yes! Fear. He's afraid.

"Tell me what ye heard or I swear –"

I push him off and smile at him. He doesn't know what to think of this. I sense the Regulators that have been following at a distance closing in. They no doubt saw Gunderson's display and assumed, as did he, that I had discovered something. As I pat down my coat, I give a hearty laugh and slap a confused Gunderson on the shoulder.

"Ha! That's a rich one, old friend! And bonus points for effect, grabbing me and all. Really sold the bit!"

"What are ye on about?" asked Gunderson, wide-eyed as he takes a step back. The Regulators, too, take a step back, realizing the situation.

"All that time in others' minds done cost ye yer own, hadn't it?

I move in close, swinging my arm around Gunderson's shoulders, turning us away from the onlooking Regulators. Gunderson pulls himself inward, not sure what to make of this. I lean in close, which does nothing to comfort him either.

"Listen to me very carefully," I say to him in hushed tones. "I did hear something – I think I know where the rebel base is or at least how to find it."

Gunderson starts to pull away, but I hold him tight. "But if ye know –"

"Shh! If I tell the Regulators, they will kill everyone inside."

"And why should I care what happens to 'em?"

I play on that fear I sensed in him. I may not be able to read his thoughts but I know it was there. "If the Queen discovers I am not misleading her, if I am actually leading her to the rebels, then what use will she have for you?"

Gunderson looks a bit confused at this, so I elaborate.

"You are only here to make sure I am not lying to the Queen. If I prove I am not, then you are as good as dead!"

This revelation causes Gunderson to perk up. I can see the wheels turning now. He knows this to be true. This is my only play – my only chance to save the lives of these rebels. This time. I just have to get Gunderson on board.

"Listen, I know we haven't always gotten along and you feel I betrayed you. But keep in mind, you betrayed me also, 'friend'. That makes us even where I'm concerned."

"And why should I listen to ye, Littleton? Why should I believe ye?"

"Consider this: you now have confirmed what you once only suspected – that I have an ability. That's how I held my own in your crew. That's how I gained you a lot of money! You also know what happened in the alley that day and that I wasn't ditching you."

Gunderson stares me up and down, contemplating this new development. Even without the use of my abilities, I can tell he is weighing his options. Follow the Queen and perhaps lose his life in the end for what he knows. Or follow me and perhaps gain riches and save his life. Maybe a life on the run but a life nonetheless.

I move in close, turning myself to face him fully. I lock eyes with him, forcing him to break his thoughts and concentrate on me.

"I have never betrayed you, Gunderson, and yet you did betray me. You owe me. And if you repay me here and now, I will help you escape the grasp of the Queen."

The Regulators have noticed we stopped and are no longer laughing. They are slowly making their way through the crowd again toward us. I look over Gunderson's shoulder at them approaching. They catch this and start moving faster, almost frantically. Gunderson has not moved, his eyes still trained fully on me. I have no clue what he is thinking now nor what his decision will be.

Two Regulators grab either of my arms, pulling me from Gunderson and inserting themselves between us.

"What's the hold up? If you know something you had better – "

As one Regulator berated me, the other one was lifting a

weapon to re-educate me as to my place. But just then, Gunderson snaps out of his gaze and addresses them, much to my surprise.

"Hold, HOLD! He ain' knowin' nothin' just yet. I was threatenin' him the same as you is all. He was convincin' me he didn' hear nothin' an' I believe 'im."

"Are you certain? Because if he's holding out on us –"

"I'm sure. Littleton never could lie ta me, not truly. I could always see right through 'im, I could."

Gunderson eyes me and I almost believe him. Maybe he did know me better than I thought. Maybe he has his own agenda, I don't know. But for today, he is an ally.

"Fine. Then we come back tomorrow. Thanks to this little display, it seems we have cost you your advantage."

"If I may, sir," I say to the Regulator, "you may not have ruined this day yet. We are known here. We can convince doubters you were merely accusing us of some crime or another."

"Go on."

"The thing is, to sell that story, we have to truly be on our own. No following behind us every step of the way."

"That's true, it is. We won' find nothin' with you lugs lumbering about. Even with Littleton's, er, *skills* we'd be cut off long before we reached anythin' substantial."

Gunderson never ceases to amaze me. He falls right into place, backing up my story. Still, I'm wary of his motives. He is nothing more than a means to an ends at this juncture.

The two Regulators confer before agreeing to leave us the night. Only after assuring us that every exit from the Ruins is guarded, so if we attempted to leave we wouldn't get far. As they leave, Gunderson pulls up beside me and reciprocates my earlier gesture by proceeding to drape his long arm across my shoulders.

"Now, let's go find us some rebels!"

This is not the path I imagined for myself nor the manner in which I sought to learn of my past. But this is the path laid before me. I am a prisoner of the Queen of New Southampton, set forth to do her bidding at the peril of countless others. I have staved off this great offense for now and have rekindled a mutually beneficial partnership. Still, I am ultimately at the Queen's mercy, but this shall not be my final fate. Whether it takes me a week, a year or a lifetime, the Queen will fall at my hand.

THE PISTOLEER

by
Chris Magee

Lord Basil Faulkner woke with a start; he looked around the room at nothing but total blackness. His right side was very warm while his left side was chilled; his right arm was also numb. A sliver of light appeared to his left and grew slowly wider as the door to the hallway was pushed quietly open. Rajesh, his valet, silently slipped into the room. “My lord, it is time to wake up; there is much to do today.”

With a grunt, Basil pulled his arm from under the sleeping woman beside him and spun around to sit on the edge of his bed. He absently reached for the black leather eye patch he kept on the stand next to the bed and covered the empty socket his right eye occupied in an earlier time. Rajesh offered tea that was readily accepted and downed very quickly. Rajesh set down the tray, moved to the window and opened one curtain to allow a green tinted light into the room, but not enough to arouse the remaining occupant of the bed. He made a hurried exit. “Breakfast in 15 minutes, my lord.”

Basil grunted again and set the empty tea cup onto the stand and made his way to the water closet attached to his bed chamber and looked into his mirror. He opened the curtains to allow the natural light in and stepped into the stream of warm water. The almost unlimited supply of hot water was the one thing he could be grateful for after the nanites ate or otherwise destroyed the previous century's technology and reverted the world to steam power. He stepped out of the shower as more light flooded the small bathroom and stood before the mirror. Aside from the patch over his eye, he was not displeased with what he saw. Standing at just over 5 feet 8 inches, he was slightly taller than his contemporaries and he credited his American birth for that. Muscles tightened and rippled under the skin as he yawned and stretched in front of the mirror.

He stepped back into his bedroom to find the woman hadn't stirred, but his clothes for the day were laid neatly over a large leather chair. He quickly dressed in black slacks with matching black jacket over a white high collared shirt and red waist coat and tie. He pushed his feet into a pair of highly shined black shoes and slipped his white spats over them. He leaned across the bed and kissed the head of the woman still in bed; she made a soft sound and pulled the covering blankets tighter over her body. He walked to the door, stopped and took a final look at the head of copper tinted hair covering the pillow and slowly closed the door.

Lord Basil ate a quick breakfast of eggs and fresh fruit, a rarity in this day and age and headed for the door. Rajesh was waiting for him, handing his lord his overcoat, which was put on promptly, then his mask and goggles. His top hat went on last as he took his cane from his valet. He didn't need the cane to walk, but it made him feel better to have the weight in his hands. Rajesh opened the door and Lord Basil stepped out into the green tinted fog as he walked across his small garden to the waiting steam carriage. A man in tweed breeches and a matching cap opened the door and bowed. "Good morning, m'lord".

"Good morning, Jeeves" Lord Basil replied. Both men knew the man's name was not Jeeves, but Lord Basil was considered kind to his staff, so he was indulged.

As he was climbed into the steam carriage, a low but loud blast pierced his ears and the earth shook, knocking him to the ground. Not stunned at all, he made sure his gas mask was still in place and crawled to where Jeeves was splayed on the ground, barely conscious. He checked the man for injuries as Rajesh rushed from the house, frantically pulling his mask over his face as he sprinted for his master. Basil and Rajesh helped the slowly recovering Jeeves to his feet and ensured his mask was in place. All three looked towards the palace to see black smoke mixing with the ever-present green mist

The ride to the Ministry of Transport was relatively uneventful with crowds of people staring off into the distance; trying to guess where the explosion had occurred and what might have been the cause. Lord Basil disembarked the carriage in front of the Ministry and climbed the stairs as Jeeves putt-putted down the street. He walked into the Minister's offices, took off the mask and goggles, his top coat and hat, which were taken by an attendant, and swiftly walked to his office near the back of the building. He took a seat behind his desk and took a deep breath before releasing it in a deep sigh. A comely young woman brought a cup of steaming tea in to him as he got settled. "G' day, m' lord".

"Good morning Emily. Anything I need to be aware of this fine morning?"

Emily gave him a quizzical look before responding. "Yes, m'lord. A post arrived for you early this morning, from the Castle, before the…" Emily held out a large red envelope bearing the seal of the palace in a very small, shaking hand.

Lord Basil spoke in a soothing voice. "Before the explosion? Do we know what that was all about?"

"Not really, m'lord. I hear it told on the street that terrorists attacked a Regulator office near the market square, but I don't know that for sure."

"That will be all Emily, you may go back to your duties." Emily left Lord Basil's office quickly and quietly, pulling the door closed behind her.

A red envelope meant only one thing, something very big was coming into the city, or something was leaving the city and it explained, to some degree, the explosion of this morning. Being the Deputy Minister of Transport for Rail, he knew that food and coal were brought into the city from places from far away, he also knew the only things that left the city was waste and misery. Garbage, to the extent possible, was reused or recycled within the city. The city was rife with crime, but was home to only a small jail in each district, and the royal dungeon. Criminals were deported from the city, that is to say, they were enslaved by the Queen and lived very short, unpleasant lives in servitude, and died a very slow and violent death.

He opened the envelope and poured its contents onto his desk. He quickly looked around to ensure no-one was close, and then shook his head as he realized he was in his office with the door closed. He read the words on the page to find his assumptions were correct. There was a shipment of fresh citrus fruit coming by ship next Tuesday, to land in what remained of Portsmouth, in the Off-Limits zone. A special train would need to be run that night and he made note that the port rail terminal would need to be visited early next week. The fruit would make it to the tables of the Queen and her nobility, but not make it to the common people on the street; well, some of it will make it to them.

The next page contained two lists of undesirable criminals that were being exiled from the city. The first list contained names of common criminals: thieves and robbers of all sorts, blasphemers and the like. He read this list very quickly; they were headed to the farms in the west where they would lead a relatively pleasant life of servitude, if they behaved themselves. The second list was the one he was interested in; these poor souls were headed for the mines in the North. This list was made up of the killers, the rebels, those who would oppose Her Majesty and those who had possession of technology from the Time That Was. This list was made up of those who the Queen feared. He read this list very thoroughly; most were the dregs of the city, people whose absence would actually make the city a much better place to live, for everyone. Then he came across the name he was looking for. Dr. Moshe Rabin.

Dr. Rabin was an undergraduate assistant to Dr. Fulbright during his days teaching at the University. But today, Dr. Rabin was more a thorn in the side of the Queen than an educator. He preached that God was mightier than the Crown and humanity should strive to topple the Crown and live as one people, with equal rights and privileges to all. He was also working on making the Creeping Green a free energy source to all and that threatened the Queen's death-grip on the kingdom.

Basil carefully folded the papers and replaced them in the envelope and put the package into his jacket pocket. He put on his outer wear, except for the mask and goggles and made his way to the outer office. “Emily, I’m not feeling well today, I’m a bit shaken up by the events of this morning and I'm going to go home.” He left the office and walked up a flight of stairs to the office of the

Minster of Transport. He walked past the secretaries and into Lord Stonebrook's office. As the Minister of Transport, Lord Stonebrook was required to meet with the Queen on a regular basis; this explained his absence from the office this morning. He placed the red enveloped on the desk and walked out.

The sky was still fairly dark as midmorning approached. Lord Basil exited the Ministry of Transport building and headed home. Rajesh showed little surprise as the gate to the garden opened and his Lord came strolling up the walk. He opened the door for his Lord and showed more surprise as Lord Basil walked into the foyer without wearing his mask and goggles.

"Lord Basil! Your mask! The Creeping Green!"

Lord Basil touched his face and realized he'd walked all the way home from the Ministry without wearing his mask, which was still safely tucked in the pouch at his side. He knew that he could exist within the green mist that permeated the city with no ill effects, but it was foolish of him to forget to wear his mask; someone could have seen him and reported him to the Regulators of Discord as a mutant.

They both brushed the incident aside as they headed towards the library. Once in the library, Basil moved to the fireplace and pushed three bricks in sequence until a shelf slid aside, revealing a stairway leading into darkness. They descended the stairs by torchlight into a small laboratory. A short, bald man was toiling away at a large chalk board, concentrating very hard on a complicated problem that covered the entire board. Basil cleared his throat as he approached the scientist.

"Ah, Basil, I didn't hear you come in."

"Good morning, Professor. I was wondering, do you know a Dr. Moshe Rabin?"

"Mo! Oh dear, yes. I know him very much so. We both worked for Dr. Fulbright, oh so many years ago. I was an idealistic graduate student of the good doctor; Mo was an undergrad that helped us out. I think he took my place working for Dr. Fulbright when I earned my doctorate and went to work for the Crown. Why do you ask?"

"Your dear friend Mo? He is being sent to the mines."

"The mines? He's an expert in food production; why wouldn't he be sent to the farms?"

"You don't seem surprised he's being sent anywhere, Doctor?"

"Forgive me, my lord, but Mo was always in trouble of one sort or another. He is a first rate scientist, but he lets his mouth run away with him, if you know what I mean."

"Hmmpf, sounds like so many people today. Is the Beast ready to go?"

"The Beast is ready to go, I've got extra cylinders of the gas, but I'm working to refine the gas so you can get more power. I've heard someone has come up with a way to refine it so it turns blue, but I haven't figured it out quite yet. I'm going aloft tonight, after dark and after the tide comes in, so no one will see."

"Go aloft, Professor, but wait for me there. Do not return until we've spoke up there."

"Yes, my lord."

***

With Rajesh's help, Lord Basil doffed his overcoat, waistcoat and slacks. He dressed in baggy black pants tucked into flat black boots and a loose fitting black tunic with a high collar. Next came a leather belt, with shoulder strap; several leather pouches were attached. Lord Basil walked to a cabinet mounted on the wall, reached in and removed a revolver with no cylinder and broke it open. He reached into the cabinet again, pulling out a blackened cylinder and loaded each port with a bullet containing a small charge to propel a small brass dart containing a brownish liquid. He slid the cylinder on the mounting spire and closed the revolver again. Revolvers, guns of any sort, were rare in this time and place; only the Regulators of Discord had them, and then, only the officers, but he owned three himself. These were illegal of course, but so was his work. He slid the revolver into a holster mounted on the right side of his belt and took a seat on a stool beside the cabinet. Rajesh came behind him and tied a bandana around his face, hiding this nose and mouth. This was tucked into the tunic. Lord Basil removed the eye patch from his right eye. Dr. Spencer placed his hand on Basil's forehead and pushed his head back. Into the empty socket, Dr. Spencer carefully manipulated a small brass orb that fit into the cavity perfectly and the eye lids blinked involuntarily. What no man could see were two small probes emerging from the back of the orb and attaching themselves to the optic nerves, providing sight where there was none. The mechanical eye gave Basil a headache, but the ability to see where there was no light was invaluable in his line of work.

It was growing dark outside as the three men pushed The Beast up a slight incline to street level behind Lord Basil's residence. Rajesh opened a small window on the door to the street and looked both ways, verifying no one was around. When he was satisfied, Lord Basil mounted the blackened brass machine that sat low to the ground on two wide tires. Rajesh placed a wide brimmed black hat on Lord Basil's head and the transformation from Lord of the Crown to the Pistoleer was complete. He pushed a button on the handlebars and The Beast came to life. He turned the front wheel to the right and silently rode the machine into the darkness and the ever present green mist.

He rode The Beast along narrow streets until he came upon the open air market in this district and caught sight of a squad of eight Regulators of Discord, at which time he ducked into a narrow alley, sped to the end. He pressed another button on the handlebars and a section of wall on the left opened by sliding to the left and he drove the machine into the hole. He was greeted by a steep ramp descending into the darkness, gradually leveling as it joined with the remains of the original city's underground rail system. Very few living people knew about the underground rail and fewer still dared to venture into its depths.

The ride along the abandoned tracks was rough, but he knew he was coming to his destination. He saw light up ahead and placed the wheel of the machine against the wall; giving the machine more power, it slowly climbed until the back tire was the only remaining point in connection with the ground. He gave a little more power and the back tire also gripped the wall and he climbed very slowly, turning back down the tunnel until he found what he was seeking. A small alcove had been built into the wall for the safety of rail workers many eras ago and was used for maintenance before the Creeping Green. He turned the machine to face where he'd come and shut the power down. He dismounted the machine and checked the fuel cells; one was expended and another was less than half used with the third and fourth remaining full. He popped the expended and the partially expended cells from their cradles and replaced them with full ones from a saddle bag on the machine. He didn't know if he would need all the cells full, but it was always better to be safe than to be sorry.

He adjusted the brass orb in his right eye socket and peered toward the light. No train was coming, but he could see the bright red jackets of the Regulators, and he could see the light blue arm bands that identified these particular Regulators as members of an elite squad that dealt exclusively with prisoners of political concern.

From his days working in the Ministry of Transport for Rail and uncounted hours of exploration, he knew where this track led, as well as all the other underground rail tracks. This track led to the mines far to the North and was a death sentence to anyone making this journey not associated with the Regulators of Discord's special unit.

In the distance, from whence he'd come, he heard the unmistakable sound of steel wheels on steel track. He pushed himself back against the machine as the locomotive, pulling a tender car, two passenger cars, six freight cars modified to transport human cargo, and a caboose, went whistling by him. The train slowed and finally stopped with the first two of freight cars lined up perfectly with the loading platform. Blue armed Regulators flung open the doors of the cars and started pushing a waiting group of prisoners into them. When the doors were closed again, the trained inched up and when the next two cars were lined up, the process was repeated.

Before the process could be completed for the third and final time, The Pistoleer leapt onto the track, jogged the short distance to the caboose and climbed the outside until he was on top. He pressed his body against the cupola as he peered around the corner to watch as the last batch of prisoners was loaded. The train edged up until the caboose was lined up with the loading platform and four Regulators climbed aboard the caboose while the rest moved along a well-lighted hall that terminated at a staircase that led to the only major Regulator of Discord building outside the walls of the Iron Palace.

The lights were doused as soon as the platform was emptied and the train started its long journey to The Mines. The Pistoleer carefully climbed down the ladder to the platform at the rear of the caboose, unholstered his revolver and flung the door open, surprising the Regulator's inside. He aimed the weapon at the closest Regulator and squeezed the trigger, sending the non-lethal dart into the man's chest. The needle pierced skin and the sedative instantly rendered the man unconscious. He fired a second time at another Regulator before any of them could react. Another Regulator hit the floor as he fired a third time. The fourth Regulator lunged at the mysterious man in black who appeared out of nowhere. The Regulator tackled the Pistoleer around the waist, pushing him back against side of the caboose, driving the air from his lungs. The Pistoleer brought the butt of the big revolver down, landing a hard blow between the shoulder blades of his attacker. The Regulator let loose a howl of pain, backing away from the Pistoleer. The Regulator, tears in his eyes, snorted and prepared for another charge. The Pistoleer leveled the revolver at the big man and squeezed the trigger a fourth time. The Regulator staggered and charged the Pistoleer again, but was met with another dart and unconsciousness. The Pistoleer leaned heavily against the wall, breathing deeply as he calmed himself. Once back in control of his faculties, the Pistoleer broke open the pistol, removed the cylinder and replaced it with one from his belt. The partially empty cylinder taking the full one's place in a leather pouch on his belt.

He searched the unconscious men until he found what he was looking for, keys to the freight cars. He stepped out onto the platform, climbed on top of the caboose and crawled his way to the first of the freight cars. Sliding between the cars, he peered into the darkness, his brass eye allowing him clear vision. "Dr. Rabin, are you in here sir?" He was met with a rush of people to the back of the car. "Is Dr. Moshe Rabin aboard this car, please?" Pleas for freedom were all that greeted him.

He climbed to the top of the car and dropped between the two cars again and pleaded, "Dr. Rabin, are you in here, sir?"

"I am. Who the devil wants to know?"

"Names are unimportant at this time, but we must get you out before the train leaves this section of tunnel, after this it straightens out and the conductor will be able to hit much higher speeds."

"I don't make it a point to join strangers on foolish quests, my good man."

"Given your circumstances, I beg you to reconsider."

Dr. Rabin hesitated a moment and said, "I've reconsidered and I shall acquiesce to your demands of me."

The Pistoleer worked the key into the lock, springing the tumblers inside before dropping the lock onto the track where a train going in the opposite direction would be and strained to get the big side door open. The train was making a series of very slow left hand turns and the door was on the right side; the conductor had no way of seeing what was happening to his load. Once the door was open, prisoners leapt to their freedom and headed down the tunnel in both directions, some the way they were heading and some the way from whence they came. Dr. Rabin was hesitant to jump, but The Pistoleer took him by the arm and jumped with him onto the track. Letting go of the scientist, The Pistoleer ran along the train and handed the keys to a young man in the last freight car after soliciting a promise to free the prisoners in all the cars.

Leading Dr. Rabin back down the track, past the now darkened loading platform, The Pistoleer pulled him up, into the alcove. The Pistoleer advised the scientist to hold tight around his waist as he started The Beast and jumped the machine back onto the tracks.

They sped down the little used tunnels for what seemed like miles before The Pistoleer slowed the machine to a stop and dismounted. He reached into the saddle bags again and produced a leather gas mask with brass rimmed goggles and handed them to the scientist. "You should put these on, doctor."

"What about you, good sir?"

"I have no need for a mask or goggles, the mist bothers me not."

"Impossible!"

"Improbable, but not impossible! You, as a scientist should know not to limit the capabilities of any subject matter. We will discuss this further, once we're aloft."

The doctor donned the mask and goggles and was astonished his benefactor had no problems breathing once they popped out onto the street and sped off into the green-tinted darkness. Masked and goggled citizens of the city made way for the brass behemoth as it traversed the city streets.

After some time, they found themselves in a semi-abandoned industrial area with many warehouses and iron skeletons reaching into the night sky. Into one of these empty caverns of commerce they rode. The Beast slid into a freight lift and the Pistoleer pressed a button and the lift began to move. The Pistoleer dismounted and encouraged the scientist to do as well as the lift came to a sudden stop. "Now we climb, my good doctor."

The Pistoleer pulled a lever on the lift to prevent it from descending without him and led the doctor to the stairs. They ascended several flights before coming to a ladder leading to a hatch in the ceiling. With a turn of the crank, the hatch sprung open and they climbed through, into a chamber with another hatch. The Pistoleer closed the first hatch before opening the second and climbing through. They climbed into an area, with nicely upholstered chairs that were bolted to the floor, and closed the hatch. The Pistoleer pointed to a chair on his left and took the one right next to it and started flipping switches as a panel lit up like Christmas and the room started to vibrate ever so slightly. The room began to tilt and rise as the man in all black pulled back on a lever.

Finally the small airship was free of its tether and began to rise quickly, heading into what seemed like an endless cloud. Around 2500 meters in altitude the airship broke the cloud cover and the skies were severely clear and the stars sparkled brightly, except for a couple of very dark blots against the sky. One of these dark spots was their destination.

The small airship maneuvered slowly until it came to be directly below a big dark spot in the sky that shimmered around a much larger airship. Manipulating a pair of levers and several dials on the panel, the airships met with a dull thud and clank. Servos activated and the airships were mated. The Pistoleer moved to the wall behind the scientist and slid a panel aside revealing another room, the size of a closet containing a ladder and a hatch in the ceiling. He climbed this ladder and turned the crank on the hatch and pushed it open. Reaching out, he was about to knock on the hatch above, but it was already opening. A pale hand reached down and he shook it. Sliding back down the ladder, The Pistoleer motioned for the doctor to come forward. The doctor slowly climbed the ladder and disappeared. The Pistoleer followed him up the ladder to find Drs. Spencer and Rabin hugging and slapping each other's backs as would old friends who never thought they would meet again. "Where are we?" Dr. Rabin asked.

"We're aloft," answered The Pistoleer.

"Aloft?"

"Yes, we're about 3000 meters above the city, in a self-contained airship. This will be your new home for the time being."

"Are, are we alone? Can they get to us?"

Dr. Spencer answered, "We are not alone. If you look out the portholes of this airship, you will see several, uh, for lack of a better term, dark spots, in the night sky. I believe these are other airships that are using the same kind of screening we are using. You can't see them in the daylight, but they appear as dark spots against the stars."

"Are they the Crown's?"

"Our contacts within the Ministry of Transport haven't said anything about them, so we don't think so. We believe the Regulators do have airships, but cannot climb this high and don't have any screening capabilities."

"Dr. Rabin, Dr. Spencer will get you settled and when you're feeling up to it, he will get you working."

"I can't stay here, as much as I appreciate your help, I just can't. I have important work to do back in the city."

Looking annoyed, The Pistoleer stated, "I don't think you understand. You were being sent to the Mines; people don't come back from there. They die a slow, horrible death there. The Queen makes sure of it."

"But it is the Queen that I'm working on. Not Queen Anne, but the true Queen, not only of New Southampton, but of the British Empire in its entirety!"

"No one in the true Royal Family survived the wars, otherwise the true heir to the throne would have stepped forward and claimed his rightful place."

"Untrue, my good man," Dr. Rabin started, "there is one true heir left to the throne. In the late 1800's, the second in line to the throne fathered a child, out of wedlock. To avoid a scandal, the mother was, sadly, murdered and the child sent away. I've traced the bloodline; I know where the true Queen is. If my information is correct, the young Queen doesn't even know she is Queen, but rather, just another urchin, struggling to survive in this world."

"If what you say is true, Dr. Rabin, then you must allow me to help you. I have many contacts within the Ministries and outside the city as well."

Dr. Rabin nodded slowly and the Pistoleer gazed out of a window of the airship. A member of the Royal Family lives!

The End…..for now!

THE BRIDE OF DR. BRAVO

by

Jaime Ramos

Dr. Bradley Wintersmith leaned down and listened to Salomé's raspy breathing. The dark green veins of radiation poison were now evident and pulsated under Salomé's nearly translucent skin. The green lines ran the course of her neck and face, into her hairline and disappeared into the dark shock of honeyed hair. Salomé ran a fever for three days. She seemed close to death.

"Je ne veux pas mourir aujourd'hui."

"Don't say such things. You will stay here with me."

"Bradley, please don't plant roses on my grave," her broken voice elevated, "they remind me of your sister. *Ne moi permettez pas de mourir cette voie Bradley.*"

"You will outlive us all, my dear. Don't give up. Please. I need you."

Bradley held Salomé's head and stared deep into her voluminous eyes. He smiled and then placed his lips against the woman's cheek. From the moment that Bradley had laid eyes on her, he had loved Salomé. He thought that maybe, he had always loved her. Bradley's sister had arranged the engagement from the first, and Bradley knew instantly that sweet Salomé was the love of his life.

The Creeping Green, however, was nearly victorious. Bradley needed something new and more powerful to stem the tide of her poisoning. Bradley stared around the room at the beakers and the tubing. He needed more of the compound. He needed more chemicals or--

"Ne moi permettez pas de mourir cette voie Bradley."

"You need to have faith my dear. *I will not allow you to die.*" Bradley would not hear that sort of talk. When Salomé spoke of her death, Bradley became afraid beyond imagination. The woman was so brave and so bright and altogether beautiful. When she said such things, Bradley thought he would go mad. Today seemed to be the last vestige of Salomé's hope. She would die if he didn't do something.

He pulled the dark brass syringe and began injecting the antidote into her neck and watched as Salomé's eyes closed. The woman's body twitched as the antidote filled her.

He could feel the heat of her fever and it was rising.

The antidote was one of many things Dr. Bravo had stolen over the last six months. The price on his head was rising. That didn't matter to Bradley. The damnable Creeping Green had taken so many in the city over the last few months.

"Voulez-vous toujours vous marier avec moi?"

"You are acting silly today my Salomé. We shall marry and live a life of prosperity. No one and nothing shall stand in our way."

New Southampton had become a place of death - a great mausoleum filled with crime and the infected. The woman's breathing stayed shallow and Bradley wiped the sweat from her brow. The antidote took what little effect it could, and the woman finally slept.

Bradley stood and moved away from the bed and Salomé, who slept and twitched as she ached all over. The humming of the steam-registers radiated something like heat into his small cottage. The cottage was covered in a dark gray plaster. The roof was covered in tan rectangular layers. There were white lines of intersecting dark grout that held the stones together.

Bradley stood and moved around his cramped bedroom. He moved to the secret closet where his work-bench and tools were hidden. Bradley entered the hidden room and found the brass and leather trunk. He opened it and began pulling out the work clothes that were dark and reinforced.

The breeches were dark leather with brass patches and deep

pockets. He put them on and tightened the wide leather work belt. The brass rings on the belt held in place bangles of little gadgets and widgets. Bradley fastened nylon tape on each ring and locked them in place. He then pulled leather greaves from the chest and fastened them over his knees and locked them into place over his shins. Bradley was never much of a fighter, but court-life had imposed certain gentlemanly behaviors that the scientist had embraced.

Bradley grabbed his woolen black shirt and tucked it neatly into his breaches. Bradley had fashioned arm greaves out of hardened grey leather and he strapped them into place over wrists and elbows. The elbow pad on his left arm held a spring loaded blade that Bradley hadn't used yet, but he figured it was only a matter of time. It was just a matter of time before Major Aldridge and his Regulators of Discord caught up to him. Bradley had heard a rumor that the Queen had actually pulled Sir Theodore Riggle of the White Hawks out of moth balls. Sir Theodore was a beast of a fighter and Bradley had been on the other end of the practice mat facing him many times.

Bradley Wintersmith left his lab by the sky-light and entered the cityscape as Dr. Bravo. He was wanted by the government for his many thefts and he knew what sort of punishment he would receive. There was no betrayal higher than betraying his Queen, betraying his sister, his own blood.

Dr. Bravo slid down the black tiled forty-five degree roof and as his steel-toed boot caught the edge, he activated his pneumatic jump boot ejection system. The compressed air whooshed out from the ejector port and Dr. Bravo blasted thirty feet into the air and flashed through the night sky. Bravo was free of this identity of Bradley Wintersmith; he was free of the enslavement that pressed down on him like a tidal wave.

Bravo reveled for a moment as he felt his trajectory change and he waved his arms to help him glide to the top of the bell-tower housing on One Twenty-two North Marne Church of the New Reformation. Bravo reached out and landed on the bell-tower housing and crested the roof like an eagle on a cliff's edge. He pulled his dark cloak tight around his torso and scanned the streets looking for concentrated clouds of the Creeping Green. He held his

Blackthorn in his left hand as he descended the bell-tower and rampart and sprang out onto the heavy clothesline that the priests had rigged. He was light as a sparrow and he could hear the mini-turbo generate anti-graviton power down to his boots. The steaming brass device was strapped to the bottom of his back. The quantum field that the device generated not only made Bravo light as a feather, but the field also seemed to improve Bravo's speed as well. The quantum field was composed of electromagnetic and gravitational forces.

Dr. Bravo ran atop the clothes line, and his boots glowed blue and steam pushed out from under his cloak and top-coat. He normally preferred less dramatic leanings but he was in a hurry. The night gave very little relief from prying eyes when one's boots glowed purple and blue and black.

It was half-past ten and very few people were on the streets of New Southampton tonight. As Dr. Bravo leaned forward and ran, he could see a group of beggars watching him in the corners and shadows. Green lines and yellow eyes stared at him as he bounded down into the alley and bounced from a red awning.

Thirty-eight feet into the air this time and Dr. Bravo reached out with his right hand. Dr. Bravo's leather-clad dueling glove grabbed the flagpole and for a moment Bravo could see the flag of his family, or the flag of his sister one should say. The flag was red and bore a golden dragon and fineries that Bravo as Bradley Wintersmith refused to share.

The quantum field danced around the metal flagpole and Bravo bent the pole back as far as physics allowed and propelled himself through the air. Dr. Bravo had a mono-rail to catch. He had to penetrate the Constabulary's Fortress in Eastleigh before the night was out.

The Queen's Transit Platform No. 14 was deserted this time of night, and it was easy for Dr. Bravo to ride atop the steam-driven elevated train. The train had been constructed by Dr. Fulbright several years before, but had been renamed by the Order of the Queen. The red and yellow iron horse blew through the platform without stopping and Bravo chuckled. It appeared that he would have to catch the end car. Good conductors were hard to find, it seemed. Bravo knew that riding the train would shave off precious time on his journey, and he adjusted his goggles so they would stay on his face, even if his top-hat blew away.

Adjusting the quantum dialer to a wider setting, Dr. Bravo kicked on the compressed air and jetted out and above the train. He grabbed the leading rolled metal of the caboose and clung like an electromagnetic spider. Bravo's graviton bonding with the side of the train gave the train rail an extra boost of kinetic energy and the train burned through the black iron lines. He would arrive in Eastleigh ahead of schedule as the guards were changing shifts. Bravo still needed to take care; the White Hawks could still be on patrol near the parade grounds. The White Hawks were the deadliest of the Regulators of Discord. Bravo knew this because he, Bradley Wintersmith, had helped train most of the White Hawks.

Dr. Bravo landed near the northern outer wall of the fortress. He could hear clamoring and movement just beyond the wall and needed to wait for a more clandestine moment to infiltrate. Bravo knew every crevice and crack in the security, and used it to his advantage.

Dr. Bravo found the cell he'd been looking for. The prisoner inside had significant meaning. The Queen's regulators had found the man on the fringes of society. His high-tech micro-processors had been fused.

Being the Queen's brother and chief Alchemist/Engineer did give Bradley Wintersmith some access to top secret projects. Bradley was given the dubious task of reverse-engineering the transhuman leftover. The soldier was cryptic and almost lifeless when Bradley had examined him. There were small things that the soldier had said that sparked interest.

Bradley's dear sister The Queen Anne Eliza Wintersmith had taken the man away when Bradley was unable to decipher the complex coding of the man's electronics. He had been locked in the dark tower and tucked away for many months. Now Dr. Bravo had use of him.

Bravo stood outside the black-iron wrought cell door. Pressing the blade button on his Blackthorn, the six iron blades ripped out of the housing. Bravo scrambled the padlock on the cell door and entered like a black shadow.

The LED light shown like a tattoo on the man's neck and it read Captain Decker-X7 2nd Army Tenth Regimental Command United States of America.

The transhuman soldiers never had ranks and rarely had names. This one must have been special in some unknown American way. Dr. Bravo leaned down in front of the man and stared into those vacuous orbs of deadness.

"Captain Decker, can you hear me?" Dr. Bravo leaned in and put his ear very close. The soldier didn't seem to respond, so Bravo slapped Decker hard in the side of the head.

Red fire sparked in Decker's eyes and Bravo could see the lingering pain and forlorn advance. As Bravo listened, a multitude of voices blasted out of the soldier. It sounded like an electronic buzzing and Bravo listened.

"Decker X-7," the nanite infused voice droned, "I have no hard memory files of you. Who are you and what interest do you have in this unit?"

"The radiation cloud, we call it the Creeping Green, is there any known antidote for toxic diseases that result from contamination?"

Captain Decker stared into Dr. Bravo's eyes and there was something almost akin to humanity for a fleeting second. "You must have faith sir."

Bravo began to frown when Captain Decker lurched forward and clamped both hands around the Doctor's head. The Captain was strong and held him for a moment and they locked eyes again.

Dr. Bravo saw a flash of light and his head began spinning.

Dr. Bravo was filled with light. The images that flowed within his mind were filled with swirling colors and textures of which Dr. Bravo had never experienced or seen before. Bravo pulled away from Captain Decker. Bravo knew that there was something different. Bravo knew that there was something inside of him now, something strange and unique.

Dr. Bravo knew that he should kill Captain Decker before leaving him, but Bravo could not bring himself to do it. Captain Decker stared at Bravo with wonder and the Nanite Army inside Captain Decker knew that they had achieved a connection.

***

Returning to the laboratory and quarters where he spent time with Salomé, Dr. Bravo crept in and removed his uniform. Salomé's eyes and skin were so pale, Bradley knew that if the antidote failed Salomé would die within hours. Bradley knew that if Salomé died, there was little point of going forward with the life that would be left destitute of mirth. Bradley's life would be destitute of love and of warmth. Bradley simply didn't wish to live life without Salomé.

The chamber itself seemed smoky today and smaller than Bradley could remember. Bradley kept the fire going at all times. The winter was brutal, but the Creeping Green somehow found its way and wound through the city. Despite everyone's best intention.

"I have returned, my sweet," Bradley said, and Salomé opened her eyes to see Bradley. Bradley, the man she loved, stared at her and smiled oddly.

There was something different about the way Bradley looked tonight, as he returned as he always had bearing some sort of compound or medicine. Salomé tried lifting her head, but the dark tendrils of the Creeping Green made it impossible for her to move. Salomé tried smiling, but instead only a grimace of agony grew up to greet Bradley.

"I have brought you something amazing. My sweet, sweet girl." Bradley placed his hands on either side of Salomé's face. He stared into her eyes and smiled. Bradley wondered if he sacrificed too much as he could feel the microbial Army that moved beneath his skin. It moved through his blood, through his veins, and through his mind. There was nothing that Dr. Bravo wouldn't do for the one person whose heart was so close to his own.

Salomé breathed in life. Salomé was filled with deep pain and she knew that the Army of Fire was inside of her. She was filled with the dread and a fear of what might be happening inside of her flesh. Salomé could feel those millions of mechanical organisms reaching deep, deep inside her flesh. It was as if an alien had made contact with her and she felt supercharged as biomechanical energy was transferred into her. Salomé's cell structure drank the richness of this newfound energy, and the organisms began to fight off the various infections that were hidden. Salomé's eyes closed and the history of the world was revealed to her in perfect clarity. Salomé could see Dr. Fulbright. Dr. Fulbright was in his lab, tinkering with technology that had lain dead and dormant. Salomé could see that Dr. Fulbright had the best of intentions, but Dr. Fulbright could have never understood what his actions would bring to the world. Salomé could see the lab, deep under the cityscape of New Southampton. Dr. Fulbright's intentions and tinkering would unlock the mysteries and unleash a power.

***

Queen Anne Wintersmith entered the wrought iron horse-drawn carriage. Queen Anne was young and beautiful with hair the color of raven feathers. The Queen was merely 30 years old and the monarch of all she surveyed. Today she journeyed with Major Aldridge to consult the seer. The Queen adjusted her silver stole, as it was cold today in the streets of New Southampton. Rumors had risen to the streets of the city like smoke through a chimney. The messages and the innuendo had made themselves available to the Queen. There were still many citizens, clergymen, and government officials and guardsmen that still regarded the Queen as a conqueror. These rumors could lead to rebellion, and the Queen would have no part in allowing a rebellion to take root in her city. Anne had worked too hard in establishing order and law in the city, and she would not have that diminished by small people.

Inside the carriage was crimson silk which pillowed the interior. Some of the citizens called the Queen, the Queen of Red Roses, because of all the blood she had spilled in taking the city. Anne Wintersmith thought this was funny, and she used the color crimson to decorate as often as possible to reinforce this image.

She stared across the carriage at Major Aldridge. The major was a man in his late 40s. The major was robust and energetic in regards to the Queen's safety and well-being. At the end of the day, the Queen felt indifferent to the major. However, the major did have his uses and purposes. The major was devoted to the Queen and her causes, but the Queen believed that the major had his own secret purposes.

"Major," the Queen smiled, "do you think that we will find any real confirmation today?"

"I certainly hope so, Highness."

"There has been a stirring of the little people recently."

"A stirring means very little to us, Highness."

The carriage rolled through the dark streets in the creeping green fog that was thick today. A specialized gas mask had been prepared for each horse in the Queen's stables. The Queen could not afford that the carriage suddenly be disabled in the mean streets, especially with all of these stirrings that she had heard.

The seer had a small shop, an herbal shop. The Queen had heard that the shop was filled with love potions, mystical tomes, and a variety of unusual remnants of the distant past. The Queen thought that one of her servants knew the seer personally. The Queen had not spoken with the servant directly but had overheard a few conversations in which her servants had mentioned the seer and her eccentric, mystical ways. Although this sort of mysticism was not a subject that the Queen took seriously, order and discipline would be maintained in the city, as well as in her own castle.

The sign outside the shop, read "Mystical Balms, Potions and Palmistry." The Queen entered the disheveled little shop, and gazed around the room at the cluttered cabinets and dingy floors. A woman who could only be the seer herself stood behind a wooden arcane countertop riddled with sigils and numbers.

"Are you my grace?" The seer moved from behind the counter and did a small curtsy. "Tell me, are you my Queen?"

"I am your Queen."

The seer was a woman in her 40's and quite attractive, with red hair that curled and ran the length of her back and down her arms in a sea of red velvet.

"What is your name woman?"

"I am called Mistress Lissette." The seer made sure to cast her eyes down, towards the floor in obeisance of her monarch. Lissette had heard the rumors that the Queen had a terrible anger and a righteous fury that knew no bounds. Lissette had no reason to question this rumor or to find out firsthand if the rumor was true or not. Lissette wondered why someone so self-exalted would visit her tiny little shop today.

"I have been informed that it was important that I visit your shop and get my fortune read."

Lissette chose words wisely, "I'm sure that my Queen has a long life and happiness waiting for her."

"Just read the tea leaves and whatever else it is that you do."

Mistress Lissette did just that. She read the Queen's palm and she read tea leaves. Lissette spent the afternoon composing the Queen's astrological chart for the upcoming year. Lissette knew better than to try to lie to the Queen. The Queen was notorious for sensing a liar. It seemed as though the Queen's future appeared to be rocky at best, full of blood and betrayal and death. Lissette shuffled a deck of Tarot cards, and hoped that the Queen's future would be brighter than what she had previously uncovered.

Mistress Lissette laid out the cards and read the results.

"I am sorry my Queen," Lissette said a bit ruefully, "I have given you my very best, but I cannot change fate."

Lissette watched as the Queen's face changed from composed monarch to an irritated witch. "Do you really think my fate is sealed because of your parlor tricks?" Queen Anne smiled now. The smile was that of a cat revealing the fate to a mouse. "My fate is what I make it." The Queen kept smiling. "The reason why I'm here is to stop you from spreading rumors about me."

The blood drained from Lissette's face. It appeared that the Queen could hear whispers, even this far from her palace. Lissette felt light-headed as the Queen's Regulators ripped her from her chair. They gripped her and pulled her body through the shop, and the Queen of Red Roses watched in amusement.

Lissette was dragged screaming from the shop and stood in the center of the street while Major Aldridge read the charges.

"Mistress Lissette Angeline," Major Aldridge held the white paper in front of his face and above his eyes, "by your own admission you have dared to spread seditious lies about your Queen, Highness Anne Eliza Wintersmith. The charge of treason carries a penalty of death. I shall now carry out the crown's judgment in this matter." Major Aldridge lifted his heavy caliber pistol and took aim, as the woman began crying.

"The Queen wanted her fortune read," Mistress Lissette cried out. "I am not a traitor. I would never harm the Queen."

"You shall not get the opportunity."

As the Queen entered her carriage, she heard a loud popping sound, and the seer's body hit the cobbled stones of the street. She leaned out the window of her carriage and motioned for Major Aldridge. "Nail her body to the shop window."

Major Aldridge nodded and saluted as the Queen's carriage pulled away from the scene with a unit of bodyguards flanking the carriage.

The winter had been brutal and Major Aldridge saw no end in

sight. It appeared that the wrath of the Queen was only beginning to be seen.

***

Later, the Queen of Red Roses moved through the passageways and passed the alcoves and she went deep inside the castle. Anne posted a guard twenty-five feet from the secret chamber. The Queen gave the guards strict orders not to allow anyone to enter her secret chamber. The chamber was lit by three torches held in silver filigree manacles. The stonework around the chamber was draped in black. It was rumored that the black iron held within a mystical quality. The Queen knew that this was true, and she stepped on the sigil and extended her arms out to either side. She closed her eyes. The Queen began the long and intricate incantation and the stone that she stood on began to come to life. The sigil began to glow.

The incantation spun out of numbers, poems, and the Queen's own willpower. She concentrated all of her energy and all of her force into the incantation. Mysticism was not easy and required blood. The Queen pricked her left wrist with a jewel encrusted dagger and the blood flowed freely. Tiny rivulets of life essence dripped upon the inscribed sigils that surrounded the Queen's feet.

She repeated the incantation and her eyes rolled into the back of her head. There was a sticky sweet, sugary feeling of deep and abiding happiness that washed over the Queen as she felt the dark energy rise from the brazier and fill the small chamber. It wouldn't be long now.

"You hunt the betrayal," a dark voice moved through her mind, "and it leaves you drained and listless."

The Queen listened, as the voices had always been accurate before. The crimson and black energy rose up and took shape in front of her. A myriad of sigils and macabre enchantments solidified into what could only be called a shade. The shade moved forward with arms wide and smiled invitingly. The shade embraced the Queen like a child.

The Queen whimpered and tried to look up, but all she could feel were the dark tendrils entering her body, her ears, entering her mind and holding her firm.

"We shall find those who betray," the loving voice whispered. The Queen wanted to open her eyes and see the power that held her suspended twelve inches in the air. The Queen could feel that power, the power base beneath her pouring out of the sigils from a dimension beyond. The power had a name, and the darkness within her tried to whisper that name into her ear. The Queen feared knowing that name. She feared that she had gone too far in drinking of the well of shadows. The Queen was growing. She could feel a thin veil of shadow rippling through the neurons of her mind.

The shade reached into the woman's soul and knew who the betrayer was. Powers of the netherworld didn't always follow logic. These powers didn't always follow science or mathematics, but the shade reached deep into her knowledge and found a name there. The name of her betrayer was her own brother.

Bradley Wintersmith.

For the first time in seven years, Anne the Queen of Red Roses wept.

***

It had been three days since Bradley Wintersmith had administered the Nanite potion to Salomé. Suddenly the dark laboratory that Bradley had spent so much time in was filled with light, mirth, and love. The energy level that Salomé now possessed filled Bradley with hope beyond compare.

"I have missed hearing your laughter," Bradley hugged Salomé close and inspected the dress she was wearing, "now that the fever has gone and you have recovered from your illness, we can plan our wedding."

"Bradley," Salomé said in her best English, "it is as if my dreams have connected me to something bigger. It's as if a thousand voices speak to me in the night."

Bradley had no idea what Salomé was saying. He had noticed that her recovery and her way of speaking had changed somewhat. Her English seem to be improving and her small frame now glowed with health and exuberance. Bradley had no idea why this was happening. He wondered if he'd made a deal with the devil. Regardless, Bradley's sister, the Queen, insisted on throwing a grand wedding for Bradley and Salomé. The union between Bradley of New Southampton and Salomé of Paris had always made sense to the Queen and her court. The Great War had destroyed many of the other countries in the world. However, it appeared that the city of Paris had made strides in rebuilding.

Bradley was still suspicious. His sister Anne seemed to love him, but Bradley never sensed that the two of them were close. Understanding his sister was like catching smoke. The self-appointed Queen of New Southampton was difficult, vengeful, complex and intimidating.

Salomé stared up at Bradley's face. She knew he was worried. But what could be done? A summons from the Queen, the engagement party, couldn't be ignored. Salomé knew that Bradley had stolen the medical supplies that were needed for her. It was a difficult situation. Medical supplies were in short order. The world was still trying to heal. She couldn't justify Bradley's thievery, but she was glad and hopeful for the future.

Salomé had grown up in the suburbs of Paris, France. Her father owned one of the few remaining iron ore factories. Robert Mercier was famous for helping the poor, and in no time Salomé's father was elected the High Mayor of Paris. A diplomatic union with the Queen of New Southampton was a smart move for Robert.

Bradley stopped Salomé's reverie. He showed her the Dr. Bravo costume, which he had fashioned. Salomé giggled at first. The costume gave Bradley a roguish look. Gone was his brown hair and blue eyes, they were replaced with goggles and a breather mask. Bradley showed Salomé how he could manipulate gravity. The overcoat and gloves were interesting, but Salomé was intrigued by the Blackthorn. The weapon held her gaze as Bradley demonstrated its many uses.

The blade sprang forth and Bradley whirled and spun in fighting stances and Salomé smiled...he was so boyish with his toy.

The wedding would take place on the queen's airship, the "Rising Wintersmith." The airship had been constructed in honor of the queen's birthday the year before. It had been hardly used. The Queen had arranged for a wedding rehearsal in the morning and then in the evening, the actual ceremony. The entire city would attend.

Perhaps Salomé was wrong about Bradley's sister, the Queen. Somehow, she doubted it. Her dreams had told her to be wary.

***

On the day of the rehearsal and wedding, the Queen met her brother. Bradley and Salomé had dressed for the occasion and waited patiently for the Queen's procession on the landing deck of the Queen's palace. The Queen approach them, followed closely by Major Aldridge and Sir Theodore Riggle. The Queen was dressed in white chiffon and a gold brocade robe which reached her ankles. The Queen's hair fell in ringlets down her shoulders and she wore a golden broach around her neck.

It was cold outside, so Salomé had worn a fur-trimmed understated coat over her simple dress of woolen brown. Bradley wore a black tuxedo with a white tie; the same tuxedo that his sister had given him two years earlier. Salomé would dress in the Queen's private sitting room aboard the airship. Queen Anne had insisted that she would help the girl dress properly.

The airship was majestic. It was constructed of the finest light woods, polished brown and brass fittings. The giant clouds of silk like materials filled with hydrogen rose above the airship impatiently. The ramps were down and the Queen's guests began moving up the ramps to take their places. Sir Theodore put his hand on Bradley Wintersmith's shoulder. "Might we have a word?"

"Why yes we can, Sir Theodore." Bradley was surprised, but turned to face Sir Theodore. Whatever could be wrong? Bradley turned and faced the old soldier. Sir Theodore was dressed in his red, blue and white Regulator dress uniform. Sir Theodore wore his blue and red captain hat. Sir Theodore's uniform was all creases. Sir Theodore held a very large package in his hands wrapped in a black oiled towel. There were two big boxes on either side of Sir Theodore. The boxes were wrapped with red and blue paper. There could only be one thing wrapped in that towel.

Queen Anne led Salomé to the sitting room. The Queen smiled while Salomé dressed in her simple dress. The French girl's hair was brown and set simply in braids behind her wedding veil. When the two finished getting prepared, they left the room and joined the others in the main cabin.

Salomé had taken her seat at the Queen's table inside the airship. The table and the cloth were fabulous and the inside of the airship cabin was decorated in green and silver fineries. Books and pictures adorned the walls, and portraits of the family Wintersmith hung here and there. The Queen and Major Aldridge sat next to the girl and they opened a port-hole that faced the landing deck.

The Queen smiled and pointed out the window. "Please watch this, my dear." Salomé face turned white and she saw the duel unfolding on the landing pad.

"You are charged with thievery, Mr. Wintersmith." Sir Theodore moved forward, handing the bundle to Bradley and stepping back five feet exactly. Bradley opened the bundle and found his Blackthorn. "You have stolen from the Queen, your sister. Inside these boxes you will find your equipment and the other items in which you used to commit crimes of thievery and sedition." Sir Theodore Riggle drew his own weapon, a silver handled cavalry saber. Bradley began putting on his costume and looked back at the airship and searched for his bride frantically. He switched the nobs and dials and turned back to Sir Theodore. "You have this all wrong, my friend."

"You ended our friendship with your cowardly deception."

Sir Theodore Riggle was an honorable man and had served the Queen well. The situation was completely wrong and Bradley turned his head toward the airship and could see his sister, smiling through the round window. Bradley locked eyes with Salomé. Bradley had to get to Salomé. Bradley could see the airship would begin moving up into the clouds. Bradley dropped the cloth that bundled his Blackthorn. He could feel Sir Theodore Riggle slashing at his arms, and then Bradley felt the pain as he turned back to face Sir Theodore.

"No quarter, you cur," Sir Theodore muttered through clenched teeth. "Don't you turn your back on me."

"Sir Theodore," Bradley pleaded with his former fencing teacher, "they are going to kill Salomé."

"Yes," Sir Theodore raised his sword into a high guard position. "The Queen has charged me with the dubious task of killing you. I preferred a duel as opposed to an assassination. Raise guard Bradley, or should I call you *Dr. Bravo*?"

Bradley raised his guard and pressed the button on his Blackthorn. A six-inch blade sprang from the end of the Blackthorn. Bradley opened the boxes and quickly pulled out his Dr. Bravo equipment.

Bradley moved forward to engage with Sir Theodore with a ferocity that surprised Bradley.

Bradley had to get to Salomé and save her. Both men parried and reposted, swinging and blocking and moving in circular motions. There was no way Bradley could win. His secrets were laid bare and all he wanted to do was rescue Salomé from the airship.

Bradley Wintersmith could see the airship slowly rising into the air. He could see his bride's face in one of the windows and fear ran through him like icy slices of pure terror. He advanced on Sir Theodore and between clenched teeth he barked, "You do not understand, Sir Theodore…"

"I understand all too well."

Sir Theodore sprang forward and slashed Bradley's chest and rivulets of dark blood appeared through his cuffed tuxedo shirt. "I regret telling your parents that I would help raise and protect you!"

"My goodness, Sir Theodore." Bradley spun and swung the Blackthorn in a torrent of jarring, purposeful arcs. "You have never been so wrong."

As the airship began floating away from the landing pad, Salomé turned back toward the Queen and Major Aldridge. "*Quelle est la signification de cela?* Why are they fighting?"

Anne Wintersmith, the Queen, turned toward Salomé, "Bradley is a traitor, and you have both betrayed me."

"He stole those supplies for me," Salomé was desperate and tried appealing to the hateful sister. "He was only trying to cure me of my illness."

"I know that, you silly thing." The Queen smiled. "He is a thief and a traitor. His actions have inspired others. We won't allow that." Anne's eyes glowed a dark bloody amber and she locked eyes with Salomé.

Salomé could see a transformation in the voice of the queen and her eyes. Salomé tried to move and spring out of the way, but suddenly black tendrils from the nether-world wound tightly around her neck. Salomé couldn't move or breath and she felt the tentacles stick to her skin and draw blood.

"You shall never betray me again girl!" The tentacles lifted Salomé off of her feet and into the air.

The landing deck stretched up into the sky three stories and

Dr. Bravo now fought with urgency as he saw the airship moving away. He had to end this fight quickly and save Salomé. Swinging his Blackthorn and spinning with the momentum, Bravo struck Sir Theodore's left arm and greave and kicked with all his might. Sir Theodore fell back and on top a broken chimney. While Sir Theodore rolled to his stomach, Dr. Bravo activated his pneumatic jump boot ejection system. Bravo blasted into the air and out into the winds.

The crowd gathered in the streets cheered as Bravo flew out and into the heavens chasing the Queen's airship. The crowd didn't realize that Bravo couldn't actually fly, he merely made himself light with the help of his mini-turbo quantum fields. The fields that Bravo manipulated allowed him to run and jump and hit the rooftops with the precision of a flying rodent. Bravo's recent thefts had inspired the people of the street and cheered for the pneumatic avenger.

Dr. Bravo bounced onto a water-tower roof and sprang forward, keeping pace with the airship, and the crowd cheered again. They didn't know why they cheered, and the crowd couldn't know that Salomé's life was in danger. But the people of New Southampton cheered thinking that somehow Bravo brought hope.

Aboard the airship, Major Aldridge and his small unit of guards stepped back and away from the Queen. She appeared to be turning into some sort of monster and he and the guards were terrified. The Queen was screaming again in that infernal voice, "You see what happens to those who betray me?" The tentacles reached out and slammed the bride through the window of the airship with a rousing crash. Anne Eliza Wintersmith and the black, writhing tentacles now held the girl out into the open air. Major Aldridge watched in horror as the girl's wedding gown was now streaked in red blood. The airship was easily one-hundred to three-hundred feet off of the ground. The Major was unsure as to what to do, so he ordered his men to leave the room. Guests on the airship had already cleared the room and jumped out for their lives.

The Queen locked eyes with the bride of her brother, Bradley Wintersmith. She held aloft the bride of Dr. Bravo. "You will pay for your deception!"

Salomé was being held and choked over the cityscape but

managed to look the Queen in the face and said only one word, "Gladly."

The shade that had joined with Queen Anne the First hissed and flung the girl away with a power and strength that would haunt Major Aldridge until the end of his days.

Dr. Bravo moved with the speed and efficiency that his quantum field generated. He bounced and jumped and sailed through the open space. Hearing the crowd below gasp, Bravo looked up high into the sky and saw Salomé flying like a doll veiled in white. Bravo's eyes widened. He could see by the trajectory that Salomé would hit streets below him.

Angling his quantum field and dropping down onto a brick and mortar store front, Bravo allowed himself to spring off the awning and fall down two more stories.

At the same moment, Salomé hit the brown cobble-stone street with a cracking sound that made the crowd shriek. Salomé lay on the cracked stone in her blood-soaked bridal veil and dress. She looked as if she were sleeping, but Bravo could see the pool of blood forming under her neck and head.

Bravo felt a deep pain in his right leg and noticed that there was bone sticking out of his right leg breaches. He saw blood and gore erupting there. With the panic and overwhelming grief gripping him, Bravo managed to move through the gathering crowd and kneel next to Salomé. Bradley removed his mask and hat and pulled Salomé up to him. No.

No. No. *No!*

Bradley Wintersmith tried standing with Salomé's inert and unmoving broken body. Instead he slipped in the pool of blood that had gathered on the stones. Bradley banged his broken leg on the stones and he howled in pain.

He felt many hands pulling him to his feet and saw the people of New Southampton trying to help him. "We have to get her to my lab!"

An old woman wearing rags frowned, "I'm sorry lad, but the girl is dead."

No. She couldn't be *dead.*

Dr. Bravo heard the clatter of hardware behind him. Bravo turned his head to see what the commotion was, and he saw two squads of White Hawk Regulators taking aim at him. The squads of ten were being led by Captain Leo Johnson. Leo was a fine young man. Captain Leo didn't ask for Bravo's surrender. He merely gave the order…

"Fire!"

Dozens of round bullets struck Bravo and the inert body of Salomé. Some of the bullets were embedded in Dr. Bravo's costume, and some of the bullets pierced his flesh, and organs. The impact of the bullets spun Bravo and his bride in a circle, one-hundred and eighty degrees. Dozens of metal balls filled them both and they spun around like marionettes dancing to music.

They both crashed down on the street with a thud. Captain Leo and the other soldiers gathered around to examine the bodies.

Captain Leo listened and heard the labored breathing of Dr. Bravo. Leo thought that he could hear speaking, or a buzzing sound. He looked and could see the girl's eyes were filled with a dark green mist. Leo leaned closer and put a handkerchief over his mouth as he examined her. The bride's eyes would haunt Leo's dreams for years to come.

Leo was mistaken, there were dozens of bullet holes in both bodies. The villains were dead.

The crowd roared and rushed forward toward White Hawks screaming in rage. Captain Leo raised his arm for another salvo and the crowd stopped. The people of the streets knew that the White Hawks would have no problem shooting them.

Leo dispersed the crowd and began the task of taking the Queen's brother back to the castle. He lifted the bride of Dr. Bravo and summoned a carriage. The girl had been so beautiful and it was obvious what she had meant to the people of the streets. Leo regretted shooting them both, but he carried out his orders with efficiency. Besides, he knew that Major Aldridge and the Queen had been watching from the airship. Leo held onto the girl's body until a proper arrangement was made.

But deep in the recesses of Salomé's brain, the Nanite Army of Fire moved in concentric circles. The Army had already bonded with Salomé and they wouldn't give her up so easily.

***

It had been three days since the bodies were entombed north of the old lumber yard. The Queen originally wanted the two traitors to be burned, but her advisor's cautioned any dramatic show of force or authority concerning the topic. It seemed that Dr. Bravo and his dead bride had an effect on the populace.

The Queen had the bodies entombed, and very few words were said again concerning the affair.

The bioelectric energy that was Salomé's soul lay deep within the recess of the dark place. The nanites bonded with that energy and held on to Salomé's soul tightly. Eventually the Nanite infused soul that was once Salomé rose from the coffin, where she lay. The revenant that was now Salomé from the grave was seen near the spot where she and Dr. Bravo had been gunned down. Many of the people of the street swore that they saw the ghost of Salomé, glowing blue and white in the moonlight. Many said that she was coming for revenge. She had risen from the dead as the bride of Dr. Bravo, pound for pound, blood for blood.

Salomé knew that she had left her body and that she was now an apparition. Salomé haunted the streets in ghost-form. In her deep darkness, Salomé had seen Dr. Fulbright and pit. The Crater of Noxious Adversity. Thc crater had been deep within her mind as well. She had seen through the eyes of the Nanites the entire history of the world. She'd seen the Great War and all of its horrors. Now, Salomé could only see through glowing eyes. Salomé no longer had a heart to break. She no longer had the same human feelings of compassion, sincerity, or hope. Revenge drove her through the streets and she searched for her first enemy. She searched for Captain Leo.

She found Captain Leo outside a brick pub. It was close to midnight and Captain Leo left the pub alone, and as Captain Leo rounded 5th St., Salomé appeared in front of the Captain.

Captain Leo's eyes grew wide as he saw the ghost of the bride. He had held the dying woman in his arms, and now he saw the glowing blue transparent ghost standing on the sidewalk in front of him.

Captain Leo squirmed and managed to grab his pistol. "No!" The visage of Salomé stood pointing one hand, one finger, one accusation at Captain Leo.

"Captain Leo," the bride said in a completely hollow, nocturnal, preternatural voice, "you have robbed me of my husband, you have robbed me of my happiness. You have taken my life. I condemn you to death."

The ghost-bride summoned the power from the microscopic Nanite particles that were infused within her soul. A particle charge of blue energy burst forth from her eyes like lightning bolts and struck Captain Leo. An immediate black bubble of death appeared and ripped the life from the soldier. Captain Leo fell to his knees and his pistol hit the ground with a clatter. He would never draw another breath in this life. The next day, the people of the street would find Captain Leo and swear that it was the revenge of the ghost bride. The Bride of Dr. Bravo had gotten her revenge.

The next morning, the Queen had received the report concerning Captain Leo's death. It was unknown if it was radiation poisoning or something more sinister. The Queen had her suspicion, but the dark power that held her transfixed in front of her mirror told her otherwise. There was no way that someone could survive falling from such a great distance. But the dark shade of power, whispered to Anne and let her know that Salomé had indeed lived from the fall. Major Aldridge had no idea. In the end it didn't matter. The Queen would have to take matters into her own hands.

The little people in the streets were whispering again. The Queen would have to check the Tombs of the Old Foundry where the bodies had been sealed up. Anne had to see for herself.

The Queen went to the tombs, and Sir Theodore accompanied her. Sir Theodore brought an escort of thirty White Hawk Guardsman in case the street people acted out. The Queen was amazed when some of the street people actually hurled profane statements at her and Sir Theodore. The Queen understood that her popularity had taken a dive as of recent events, however she had no idea that the people had turned on Sir Theodore. The fight with her brother, Bradley, had damaged Sir Theodore's reputation. Sir Theodore, for his part, ignored the crowd that was gathering around the building. The knight escorted the Queen inside the cemetery so that the two of them could have a look at the bodies.

The tomb itself was ancient and dank. The caretaker himself, named Charles, seemed nervous and expectant of a harsh punishment. Sir Theodore assured Charles that there was no reason for him to be afraid. The round flat stones of the tomb were brown and red and black. The tunnel was formed arching in a half circle. Charles led Sir Theodore and the Queen down the sloping hallway as it wound down and down into the depths.

"I don't think that anyone's been here, my lady." The caretaker shook his head and kept his eyes down, towards the floor.

"Charles, you are a faithful citizen." The Queen smiled. The smile itself did not reach the Queen's eyes. The caretaker was still afraid. The Queen took the lead. She let the caretaker and Sir Theodore into the circular chamber which held bodies. She first found her brother's body in its lacquered black coffin. The Queen pulled the coffin from the chamber opening on the wall. Anne ripped open the coffin lid and saw the face of her dead brother. There was nothing to see here, Bradley was dead.

The Queen then moved to the next door. The door was small, circular and closed. The Queen yanked on the door and it opened with hiss. The small woman then reached into the opening and grabbed the coffin that was hidden from sight. She and Sir Theodore placed the coffin on the floor in the center of the chamber. Sir Theodore grabbed for the torches from the wall so they could get a better look. The chamber was dark and visibility was low. The Queen would not be happy until she examined the body herself.

The Queen and her knight opened the lid and found the body of Salomé lain there dead. "I knew this was all rubbish." The Queen turned to Sir Theodore and smiled. If you want something done correctly, one must get their hands dirty. At that precise moment the door leading into the funeral chamber slammed shut. It was as if all of the air in the room had fled, and hovering near the door was the bride herself.

Charles the caretaker was terrified and pointed his finger at the apparition. "It is her, the bride of Bravo!"

"My God," Sir Theodore exclaimed, shaken by the sight, "how can this be?"

Salomé hovered there in silence. She still wore her bridal gown, with the veil covering her face. Her eyes were the brightest blue and shined through the veil. After a moment of silence the bride spoke, "Charles, please leave the chamber." As if on cue, the chamber door opened, and the caretaker ran through the doorway as if possessed.

The Queen of Red Roses stood slowly, keeping a keen eye on

her adversary. “Sir Theodore. You can leave as well.” Sir Theodore started backing toward the chamber door, but was cut off by the spectral image.

“He is going nowhere…” Salomé disappeared and her image reappeared surrounding Sir Theodore. Salomé’s preternatural essence surrounded Sir Theodore, moving in and out and around, smothering him. Her ghostly presence, combined with her high-tech signature, began a series of bio electric stings that overwhelmed Sir Theodore. The shocks grew in volume and depth until Sir Theodore’s skin turned translucent and began burning. His body fell to the floor like a darkened husk.

“How dare you!” The Queen herself was not so easily frightened. She held within her being a shade, an absence of light, an abnormality so dark that she likened it to a black hole, a singularity. “You will reunite with my brother in hell!” The Shade of Elder Days took control of the Queen now and tentacles of the Abyss sprang from Anne’s head in a torrent of darkness and shadow.

Salomé watched with unblinking blue eyes as the Queen transformed into a being from another realm. The Queen’s form stretched over two meters and a black inky sheen appeared on her skin.

“You stole my life, my love, and the hope of all.” Salomé’s blue spectral form shimmered and she began filling the chamber with a bright white light. “Anne Wintersmith, who calls herself Queen, shall rule no more!”

The chamber was filled with terror as the two entities united. Magic energies based both in the nether and technology melded into one. The resulting explosion could be heard from Eastleigh to the south of Hythe-Barrows.

Many people believed that they saw the Queen again. Many people believed that the Queen haunted the shadows. No one truly knew what had happened. Many people believed that they saw Salomé on the streets of the city. Some people thought they could hear her weeping in the darkness. Time has a way of obscuring the fact from the legend. No one really knew for sure what happened to the Queen of Red Roses or Salomé.

There were many people that believed that the bride of Doctor Bravo disappeared into the Creeping Green. The people hoped that one day she would return if she were ever needed again.

The truth is that the Bride of Dr. Bravo never left the city. She stood somewhere between life and death, on the borderlands watching and waiting for her wedding. The Bride was waiting for her groom on the edge of forever.

ABOUT THE AUTHORS

David Michelinie has been a professional writer for over 40 years. He has written more than 600 comic book stories, spanning genres from westerns to war to horror to super hero. In addition to his comics work, David has published two novels, has had short stories published in anthologies (WEREWOLVES: DEAD MOON RISING) and periodicals (Spider-Man Magazine), and has written scripts for the Nicktoons animated series, "Iron Man Armored Adventures." His comic book biography of Mother Teresa won the Catholic Book Award for Best Children's Book, and his work on the acclaimed Iron Man "Demon In A Bottle" saga was awarded a Certificate Of Merit from a prestigious anti-alcoholism foundation.

Jennie Wood is the creator of Flutter, a graphic novel series published by 215 Ink. The Advocate calls Flutter one of the best LGBT graphic novels of 2013. Bleeding Cool lists Flutter as one of the 15 best indie comics of 2014. She is also the author of the YA novel, A Boy Like Me, which is a Next Generation Indie Book Awards finalist, an INDIEFAB Book of the Year finalist, and one of Foreword Reviews' 10 Best Indie YA novels for 2014. Jennie is an ongoing contributor to the award-winning, New York Times best-selling FUBAR comic anthologies. She writes non-fiction features for infoplease.com and teaches at Grub Street, Boston's independent writing center. More: http://jenniewood.com/.

Nancy Hansen is an avid reader and prolific writer of fantasy and adventure fiction for over 25 years, Nancy A. Hansen is the author of the novels FORTUNE'S PAWN, PROPHECY'S GAMBIT, MASTER'S ENDGAME and FORGED BY FLAME, anthologies TALES OF THE VAGABOND BARDS, THE HUNTRESS OF GREENWOOD, and THE WINDRIDERS OF EVERICE, novellas COMPANION DRAGON'S TALES: *A FAMILIAR NAME* and co-author of *FINDING WAXY*. Her short stories have been featured in multiple issues of Pro Se Presents, and she has a tale each in Pro Se Anthologies THE NEW ADVENTURES OF SENORITA SCORPION, TALL PULP, THE NEW ADVENTURES OF THE WHIRLWIND, and MONSTER ACES, while the E-story TO RULE THE SKY is offered as a Pro Se SINGLE SHOT. Nancy has also contributed stories to both Airship 27's SINBAD: THE NEW VOYAGES Volume 1 and Mechanoid Press' debut book, MONSTER EARTH, and the charity anthology THE LOST CHILDREN. Her first pirate novel, JEZEBEL JOHNSTON: DEVIL'S HANDMAID was a recent release from Airship 27 as well. Nancy currently resides on an old farm in beautiful, rural eastern Connecticut with an eclectic cast of family members, and one very spoiled dog.

Lee Houston, Junior is the writer-creator of *Hugh Monn, Private Detective* and *Alpha* the superhero, published by Pro Se Press.
His other creative credits include serving as the Editor-In-Chief of The Free Choice E-zine (www.thefreechoice.info) and writing numerous short stories. His complete bibliography can be found on his Amazon Author's page.
In what he laughing refers to as his "spare" time, Lee is an avid reader of pulps, science-fiction, detective/mystery stories, fantasy, and comic books.

Brant Fowler is the Co-Publisher of Last Ember Press (www.lastemberpress.com), where he writes the comic books Wannabez and The Last Ember. He won an Editor's Choice Award for his poem The Abyss while in college. The Eye of the Mind is his first published prose work. Brant was born in Georgia, raised in Arizona, South Carolina (on a wildlife preservation island), and

Kentucky, and now resides in Texas with his dog Trixie.

Chris Magee was born into a military family and lived a nomadic lifestyle until finally landing in Lebanon, MO, which he considers home. After graduating high school, Chris himself, entered the military and became nomadic once again. During his third deployment to Operation Desert Storm, Chris and his squad, members of the elite Special Airborne Ranger Seal Artillery Composite Provisional squad, part of Team 'Merica, discovered a cache of gold bullion while on a suicide mission. Being the sole survivor of the mission (making him a suicidal failure), he decided to keep the gold for himself, instantly becoming a billionaire. Chris then embarked on what he felt he was truly meant to do, be a billionaire playboy with no real job. This led to many adventures doing "special" contracts with the CIA, FBI and CBS. In his free time, Chris enjoys keeping the world safe for himself, chasing very attractive younger women and spending time with his wife and children.

Jaime Ramos is a fiction writer who resides in the St. Louis area with his wife, son, two dogs and a cat. Jaime has been writing fiction since he was a young child. Jaime sold his short-story "Exile of Avalon" in 2014. Jaime serves as Chief Editor and creator of the super-hero themed anthology "Singularity: Rise of the Posthumans," which is being published by Pro Se Productions. Jaime also is an assistant editor on the book "Legends of Pulp," published by Airship 27. Jaime is currently under contract to publish two pulp novels in 2016.

Jaime enjoys football, movies, cooking and playing make-believe with his son Thomas. Jaime has an idyllic life with wife Phyllis, who is a constant source of encouragement.

Made in the USA
Lexington, KY
09 August 2016